SEASIDE HOLIDAYS

KIM KATIL

Edited by Jill Wexler

Cover design by Kim Katil

Formatting by Other Worlds Ink

Note that this collection is comprised of three previously published stories:

Season to Shimmer (published in 2018; minor editing changes only)

Rainbows in Sea Glass (published in 2019; minor editing changes only)

Holiday Lights (published in 2019; major revisions and edits)

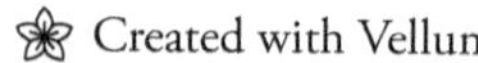 Created with Vellum

CONTENTS

ACKNOWLEDGMENTS

A writer is a creature of highs and lows, and without encouragement and support, very few books would be finished. There are many who helped me along in this process of creation.

First and foremost, I am deeply grateful for my family, who hold my heart and keep it safe from the battering storms along the way. This year has been difficult with the losses of cherished love ones. It is bittersweet to reflect on all the love that I've been given now that those lights have diminished.

Jill, thank you for keeping me on task and fixing all the things!

To my writer's critique group, thank you for being there and helping me find the path to what I am trying to say.

SEASON TO SHIMMER

One morning close to the holidays, Nolan wakes up to two surprises: a distress call from his younger brother and a beautiful man in his bed. Nolan, an art gallery owner, has always been discreet about his sexuality, but when his baby brother plans to come out at the annual family gala, Nolan wants to have his back—and that means showing up with a man of his own on his arm. Nolan knows just the man for the job.

Skylar, who owns a karate studio in St. Augustine, can't get his one-night stand out of his mind. When he runs into Nolan at his gallery he is more than happy to volunteer his services as arm candy. Out-and-proud himself with his striking blue/green hair, Skylar is all in. Their adventure means a fancy salon, family drama, lots of sex, a ninja hippo, and palm trees lit up in a very suggestive way. By the end of it, what started as a hookup might become much more.

RINGING IN THE MORNING

Nolan

The obnoxious ringtone roused him from a lovely dream involving a beautiful man who lay beneath him on the beach…. Then he realized that his arms were full of warm, lithe man. He reached for the phone, beyond irritated at the interruption.

"Yeah?" he asked, not bothering to check who it was. He was edging toward a headache and unsettled by the strange man in his bed. That didn't stop him from running his fingers through the shiny hair that lay on his pillow. He was momentarily lost in the colors, silvery blues and greens swirling through his fingers. He vaguely remembered twirling that hair around his fingers for what seemed like hours in a drunken stupor last night.

"I'm getting Den out of here and heading to my apartment," Tor bit out, anger tinging his words.

"Do you need me there?" Nolan asked, sitting up.

"Nah, I'm in the car already. Dad's being a grade-A asshole, and I don't want Den to have to deal with him anymore. I'll bring him back to my place; he has plenty of stuff there to hang out with us for a bit. Luckily school is out for the holidays. We'll just play a bunch of games this afternoon."

"How about I show up at dinner with a few pizzas?" Nolan asked, wanting to be there to support his brothers but realizing that Den and Tor needed some time to themselves. He was distracted as the beautiful man got up and headed for the bathroom. He remembered calling him Shimmer but didn't think that was his actual name.

"That sounds great, bro. I can't believe…."

"Oh, I can. But we'll discuss that tonight," he told his brother wearily.

"Hey, sorry to ask this of you, but I was at home this morning to mooch breakfast and do some laundry. Obviously, plans changed. I texted Mom, and she's gonna finish the laundry for me. Dad has a tee time at three over at the Golf Village. Think you can swing by and pick it up on your way here while he's out of the house?"

"Yeah, I'll do that, no problem. I've got ya, Tor. We'll make it through this."

As he hung up the phone, Shimmer returned looking halfway pulled back together rather than thoroughly debauched. Disappointment ran through him.

"Problems at home? Should I get out of your hair?"

"My brothers need my help, but as you heard I don't need to go over until tonight."

"Brothers?" the man asked carefully, as his face lit up with a smile.

Nolan considered him with a smirk. "Did you think I had a boyfriend waiting for me or something?"

"Or something. I really hate trying out for the role of slut in the boyfriend's bed. It's not a good look on me."

"Well, I beg to differ on one account. You lying here in my bed is a very good look on you. I think you need to reprise that role right away by coming back to bed. And to answer your question, I have a stepbrother named Victor and a half brother named Riorden. Victor is in college nearby at Flagler, and Riorden is still in high school. Their father married my mother almost twenty years ago. Here, drink this and I'll be right back," Nolan said, tossing Shimmer a water bottle from the side table as he headed toward the bathroom.

It didn't take him long to get rid of the rock that had settled on his bladder, then to wash his face and quickly brush his teeth. He returned to the bed, absurdly glad to see it once again occupied. He reached out to caress the man's cheek as he took away the half-empty water bottle and downed the rest. He went to put the empty bottle on his bedside table and had to laugh.

"One of those little anoles just hid under your hat," he said as the small lizard dove for cover. "Apparently it's a fairy lizard, because the glitter on the elf hat may blind me. I think the lizard is now fully coated in holiday sparkle."

"Hey, that lizard has excellent taste. What else could I wear for holiday night at the nightclub? Did you see that guy in the reindeer thong? With the bells? I'll have you know my elf outfit was very tasteful, and well, glittery," the beautiful man said as Nolan climbed over his lover, straddling him. The man beneath him eyed his nipple piercing hungrily as he asked, "Now that I know your brothers' names, may I ask yours?"

"Oh, right. Nolan Donovan. Sorry."

"Very nice to meet you, Nolan," he said, reaching up to take his lips in a ravenous kiss.

Nolan finally pulled free long enough to breathe out, "And yours?"

"Skylar Lopez," came the reply just as their lips began to duel again. He savored the feel of taut skin as he moved his hand down his naked chest. He was voracious as he moved his lips over Skylar's skin, working his way down to the taut nipples.

He abruptly found himself flipped over and laughed at the victorious glee in the other man's eyes. Skylar was about average height, a few inches less than six feet, but his lithe body was a masterpiece in lean muscle.

"I just needed to play with this. It's so shiny and…." With that the words cut off as Skylar explored that bit of metal enticement Nolan had pierced through his nipple and his beautiful dark eyes gleamed with passion. Nolan moaned, the other man finding and drawing out every one of the sensations that he had envisioned when he'd crafted the silver piece and then had a friend do the actual piercing.

Nolan writhed beneath the talented lips that seemed obsessed with teasing at his nipple jewelry. Damn. He knew men found it hot, but Skylar sure seemed to be into the whole thing. Maybe he should consider a few more piercings….

Skylar

Nolan lost his mind while Skylar teased his nipple. Definitely going to remember that one.

"There, baby. Yeah, right there," Nolan breathed out.

"Ah, but what about here?" he said, as his lips traced Nolan's chest. "This is some nice definition you have going on here. You're going to give me some serious cowboy fantasies as you look like you belong on a ranch."

Nolan laughed. "Thank you. I actually own an art gallery downtown. But I do a lot of sculpture work myself, and that takes a lot of strength. Sadly, no roping of cows, though."

Suddenly, Nolan rose up and flipped Skylar onto his back, then used his tongue to trace each and every one of the hardened curves on his stomach. "Your abs are driving me insane, Shimmer."

"Shimmer?" Skylar asked, momentarily distracted.

"Your hair. It's all shimmery. It's amazing, like a piece of art that draws you in and distracts. But your abs…." And with that, Nolan returned to his thorough exploration of every dip and curve, turning Skylar into a writhing mess on the bed. Until his mouth finally trailed even farther south and, in a shockingly swift move, swallowed Skylar's erect cock down to the root.

Skylar reached down to grab the man's tempting hair, which was a tousled brown that just begged to be messed up. And when the humming started, as Nolan teased at his balls with his talented hands, Skylar lost his grip and himself to the feelings that overwhelmed him until finally he shouted his release.

As he lay there and panted, Nolan eased off his cock and licked his inner thighs, where some of his spill had leaked. Maybe he would just die here in this bed from sensation overload. What was an orgasm called again? The little death? That definitely seemed accurate at the moment.

"You sure hit the gym hard," Nolan said as he continued to explore his body.

"Well, since I own Fortress Dojo and teach classes there…."

"Ah, that would explain it. Black belt? You definitely have the body for it."

"Yeah, I pushed that hard when I was in college. Did a bunch of training with people I respect and got a business degree to help with the ownership part."

"All of that and you dance like an angel. I couldn't keep my eyes off you in the club last night. How did I get so lucky?" Nolan asked as he reached for the lube bottle that had rolled out of range sometime last night while they were fumbling around in the haze of alcohol and lust. Then all thoughts escaped him when Nolan fingered his entrance. He shivered in anticipation.

"That's beautiful. Suck in my finger, just like that. Here's another one. You're doing so well, I can't wait to get my cock in there. My fingers are buried so deep; let's fit in another one."

Skylar groaned inarticulately as Nolan continued to open him up while using actual words. Words! He was so beyond that and just listened to his body as it welcomed his lover. Foil tore and he looked up to see Nolan holding the condom packet in his mouth as he carefully covered his shaft. Then he removed the shiny packet from his mouth and reached down with his other hand to stroke Skylar's cock.

"That's it, look at me. I'm about to fuck you into this mattress, hard and deep. But you tell me if something's not right, yeah? I'll stop whenever you need me to. Otherwise, I'm going to own this ass right here." And with that, he removed his fingers and gave Skylar's ass a swat. Skylar groaned again.

Nolan chuckled, deep and resonantly. "Like that, huh? Let's see how you like this." And with that he entered Skylar, pushing down swiftly and surely until he bottomed out, and then stopped.

Skylar panted through the nerves that sang as he was filled and taken, then looked up at Nolan with wide eyes. "Now! Move! Fuck me. Just like that...."

And Nolan responded, reading his body language like a master, hitting the sweet spot time and again as he filled him. Skylar's cock began to harden as he reveled in the sensations running through him. Right now he would enjoy every moment of Nolan's erotic attentions. Doubts were things to be dealt with later.

And then Nolan did something with his hips and was pegging his prostate in a raw flurry of passion and need. Skylar let himself feel everything as his cries and demands got louder and rougher.

"That's it. Tell me what you want, what you need." Nolan took his mouth in a ravenous kiss cutting off any more words. The friction against his cock was exquisite as he chased the release that rushed through his body. His body's reaction when he came was obviously too much for Nolan, who thrust deep into Skylar one last time and then stilled, panting.

PIZZA AND PLOTTING

Nolan

"So I have pizza and clothes," Nolan said as he entered his brother's apartment. Luckily for his senior year, Tor had gotten an off-campus apartment, though parking in downtown St. Augustine could be a bitch. "The laundry is still in my car and someone can run down later to get it."

"I take back everything I just said about you," Tor told him as he grabbed the pizza boxes.

"Ass," Nolan retorted.

"He really is," Julia replied. "Thanks for grabbing this stuff, Nolan. I think all my bras are in that load of laundry."

"I didn't really need to know that," he told his brother's girlfriend. "Though I'm shocked you let him wash delicates. Did he ever tell you about the incident with the jockstrap?"

"Pizza!" Den cheered as he entered the room. "Did you get sausage and pepperoni?"

"Yeah, he got you your meat pizza," Tor said with a smirk.

"Oh, shut it," Den said as he grabbed the pizza and a napkin.

"Meat pizza! I'm so there!" Byron said as he grabbed a slice.

"Hey, Byron, how's it going?" Nolan asked Tor's best friend and roommate. The two had grown up playing basketball together and been thrilled to play on the same college team.

"Much better with pizza, Nolan. So what's with the reunion? I thought you and Julia were going over to your folks' house today, Tor."

"Well, while you were out canoodling with Jazz, you missed all the fun. I stole Den from my father's wrath, then called up Nolan for support, and pretty sure I interrupted whatever morning bed activities he had going on. Which, by the way, I really don't need to know anything more about."

Byron just laughed. "I'll have you know, there was no canoodling. Jazz and I had to finish up that blog entry we were working on for the team's Christmas fundraiser to support the teen shelter. We were doing it at her place, but her internet went down so we came back here. She's just wrapping it up and posting it now. So Den is going to stay with us for now?"

"Yeah, at least school is out for all of us. That damn Christmas event is this coming weekend, and I think we need to figure out what to do about it. Den, you said Aaron agreed to come with you? And you're sure you want to do this?"

"Hell yeah. I mean we've been together for two months now. So of course he's going to be my date. I know he'd be upset if I caved and brought some girl and stuffed him back into my closet like a suit that doesn't fit or something."

Wow. His brother really went there. Nolan felt a surge of pride run through him.

"Calm down, Den. We can make this happen, but there's no going back. So you have to be sure, that's all," Nolan said.

"Yeah, I'm sure. But I'm also sure that Dad is going to lose his shit. And I don't want that to get all over Aaron either. I mean, I want to bring him with me, but I don't want him to get caught in the crossfire. I don't know how to make that happen," Den said, looking at Nolan sadly. "I get why you never pressed the issue. But… Aaron's important to me."

"I get it, and you're right. Did you already ask him? I suspect that he'll be a lot more hurt by you not asking him than by whatever madness the family will throw at you."

"Yeah, I asked him, and he said of course he'd come, even if things got ugly. I just don't want him hurt, ya know?"

"I am so damn proud of you right now, Den. We'll figure it out. And I think part of it is showing how much we are there to support you. I'll bring someone as a date this year." Nolan never had because it hadn't been worth it to press. He'd always been hesitant to do anything that might cause his stepfather to try to cut him off from his brothers. But now it was time to take a stand.

"Is that fair to whomever you bring? I mean, you're not dating anyone seriously right now, are you?" Den asked.

"Nah, but I'll make sure he knows the score." Nolan had fixed on calling Skylar. The beautiful man would be perfect for the role. Hopefully he would agree. Maybe he could offer bribes. And maybe he'd have another chance to run his hands through Skylar's amazing hair.

"You know, I think I'm coming down with something," Julia suddenly announced, then proceeded to hack and cough like an eight-year-old trying to get out of school. Which shook Nolan out of the lovely thoughts he was having about exactly how he could bribe Skylar.

"Um, Julia?" asked Tor.

"Yup. Definitely coming down with something. Won't be able to make the party. But Tor, you should bring someone with you since you already RSVP'd with a plus one. And they'll have ordered a dinner, and that really would be a shame if you didn't have someone there to eat it...."

Tor had an amused gleam in his eye as he smiled at Julia. "Are you suggesting I bring my best friend so that the food doesn't go to waste?"

"Exactly!" She beamed back at him.

"So, Byron, how do you feel about being my escort for the evening?"

Byron just shook his head and looked at Julia. "You are trouble."

"This is going to be so much fun!" Julia said, jumping up and down.

"Damn, woman, you are ten times more excited to ditch me for the biggest event of the season than you were when I asked you to go."

"Yeah, well, that big event of the season is usually boring as fuck. And damn, if I post pictures of you two, our site is going to explode. What's our next step?" Julia asked in a breathless voice.

"I think the next step is for you to take a chill pill, darling," Tor said with a resigned smile on his face. "But yeah, a bunch of pictures leading up to the big event may be a good idea. Some of Den and Aaron, me and my man here, and even Nolan and his mystery man."

"What are we taking pictures of? And why are you stealing my man here for pictures?" asked Jazz as she walked in the room.

Byron swept her up in his arms for a kiss and then solemnly informed her, "I'm throwing you over for Tor. And it's all Julia's fault."

"Explain," Jazz demanded, looking at Julia with a raised eyebrow.

"Tor's dad is being a piece of work and freaking out over Den bringing his boyfriend to the Christmas Ball. So Nolan said he's bringing a guy, 'cause we all know he's gay but he's never pushed the issue with his stepdad. And I figured it would be cool if Tor were to bring Byron, you know, as a sign of support. So Daddy Dearest can't point to Tor and tell the other two to be like him. Or blame Nolan and Den's mom for being responsible for all the gay."

"All the gay?" Nolan laughed. "And I don't think Dad will actually believe Tor is gay."

"He might not believe that, but he'll sure be unhappy if Tor brings me with him," Byron said, smirking.

"Why?"

"He's tolerated me as Tor's friend, but he really wishes I would just go away. My skin tone is a bit dark for him, and my parents far too blue collar."

Nolan gaped at Byron. "Seriously? You've been friends with Tor as long as I've been around him. And your parents are both teachers and amazing people."

"Yeah, and none of that matters to dear old dad. Your mom is the one who's always set up the play dates and then handled all the driving stuff for ball when we were in school. Your dad knew she wouldn't stand him being a bigoted ass, but that didn't mean he wasn't. He just doesn't want to look like it to the friends and neighbors."

Nolan looked at his brothers and realized that they had decided on a path that would change their family forever. Hopefully for the better, but there was no going back.

"Okay, we're all in on this thing. If Dad won't support Den, then we will. I'll talk to Mom at some point and give her a heads-up. I've never known where she stood on the gay thing, to be honest. Like I said, I was content to let that lie, because I never wanted to give Dad an excuse to cut me off from you guys. But now—"

Den rammed into him and hugged him hard. "Seriously, bro?"

"Seriously. If Dad goes all country club on us and kicks your ass out, you'll come live with me. And we'll figure out Tor's tuition if it comes to that as well."

"I've got scholarships, and my mom pays for part of it. So that won't be a big deal. I can always take out some loans myself if I need to," Tor responded seriously.

"All right, it's good to know we have a plan, but hopefully we're getting ahead of ourselves. I know your dad seriously loves you two, and I'm hoping he can get his head out of his ass. With Mom, I gotta hope she'll have our back, but it's hard to tell with her. She is so over the top in love with your father that it makes it easy for her to overlook his faults. I'm hoping she'll make a stand, and not just a quiet one. But regardless, I've got your back. Both of you. You know the gallery is doing really well, and I have plenty of room at the house."

"So we taking some pictures or what? Because these two together will be *hot*," Jazz said, and Nolan was relieved to see his brothers smile.

Julia laughed. "That's what I was saying. Can you imagine the traffic to our site?"

"Down, girl, we're not going to pretend to be gay. That's just wrong. But we are going together to the ball. I like the idea of having Den's back and making a point," Tor told his girlfriend.

"Yeah, and we're going to record the bromance of hotness," Julia retorted as Jazz giggled. The two young women did a complicated high five while the guys just groaned.

"I'll put up a statement with the pictures that while Tor and Byron aren't actually dating, they are going out together as friends to formal events this Christmas to support those who are being told they can't bring someone of the same gender or a different race," Jazz said in an excited rush.

"Okay, you guys work on the bromance of the century. I'll see if

I can get a date. In the meantime, I'm going to get to the gallery since Jasper is having his first showing and it's going to be very busy tonight. Den, you okay here for now? Is there anything you need?" Nolan said before the girls could get really rolling. He was enjoying their excitement, but it was making him feel old. And the day had worn him out already. Luckily the gallery was only open for a few more hours tonight, but it would be crowded with the Christmas activities. The Night of Lights was a huge tourist draw in St. Augustine. And while people who lived there loved to ridicule the tourists, they were the underpinning of the city's economy. So he would be polite and charming and make them all happy they had come to visit his regal lady.

"No, I'm good. Thank you so much, Nolan. Really. Oh, and give Jasper my best wishes. It's so much fun to see all of his new creations every time I come to visit. He's gonna do awesome, I just know it!"

"I'll let him know but you guys should stop by to see his full exhibit. It truly is amazing. Our clients are going to love everything he has on display. Okay, I'm going. Call if you need me."

NINJA HIPPOS

Skylar listened to his mom bubble with excitement and was glad he had indulged them both by taking this trip downtown to see the holiday lights. He had always considered it a tourist thing and avoided it like the plague, but he hadn't realized how truly beautiful the Night of Lights would be. St. Augustine was an amazing city, and the heart of it was on display tonight.

They had reached Cordova Street, and the gallery address Nolan had mentioned was just up the block. Since he was obviously busy with family tonight, this was a good chance to check out his business without any awkward meetings. The lights were strung up in an overwhelming display, framing the stately old buildings and circling the palm trees. Each storefront and business was worth a second glance.

"Oh, look at that, Sky!" Mom exclaimed at the lights outlining the gallery and the showpieces standing on display outside.

"It's amazing, Mom. Let's go inside," he said, as he guided her through the door. When he walked in, he was assailed with the enticing scents of cinnamon and apple and the sounds of softly played Christmas carols.

A young woman walked over to them, and Skylar took a minute to admire her ensemble. She had on close-fitting pants covered by a long jacket with ruffs and a flapper-style hat. The material was darkly rich and was complemented by her long, wavy chestnut hair.

"Welcome! Please feel free to look around. There are some refreshments under that window over there, and the hot cider is extra yummy tonight. If you have any questions, just let me know. My name is Lisa. Otherwise, enjoy!"

"Oh, thank you, dear. It's amazing in here! I just want to look at all the wonderfully pretty things!" his mother declared, and Skylar was thrilled to hear the delight and excitement in her voice. Sometimes he worried that she had gotten too quiet. She had been a well of strength for so long. Recently he had felt helpless when her ever-present joy in life had seemingly vanished.

She'd lost the job she loved so much when 789 Dance, the nonprofit she had been working with, had cut back on staff. He had noticed his normally vibrant and beautiful mother turn uncertain as she worked through her grief. She had loved her job and everyone at the studio. He knew that she would have been willing to volunteer there if she had been asked, but no one had reached out to her. "Sky, I must take a look at this amazing creature. Come, come," his mother declared, dragging him in tow. The delight in her voice was a balm to his heart.

As they drew closer, Skylar could see why his mom was so entranced. The sculpture was large, almost five feet. The piece was positioned at the central point to the main area, and was obviously meant to be a statement piece. The colors were dazzling and the creature was posed mid-leap with a look of joy on its face. Skylar itched to touch, but he managed to keep his hands rigidly at his sides while he walked around to the other side of the display, caught up in the intricacy of the work.

"This piece is simply called Joy," said a familiar voice, startling him. "Jasper outdid himself with this one, and it throws out lures to the passerby. Just like a certain beautiful man...."

And with that Nolan's lips brushed Skylar's cheek.

Skylar was momentarily overwhelmed by the proximity of the other man, but quickly lost that thought when he turned his face and Nolan kissed him sweetly then nibbled for a moment on his lower lip.

He looked up and saw his mother staring at them from the other side of the statue, her mouth open and her eyes wide in astonishment. As his face flushed red, she gave him a knowing smirk, then walked over to them.

"Sky, dear, I take it you know this gentleman? Or was this a piece of performance art?"

"Of course I know him, Mother! This is Nolan Donovan. He owns this gallery, and is a sculptor as well. Nolan, this is my mother, Cordelia Lopez." Skylar was proud of his ability to get out a complete sentence as he felt his skin flush from embarrassment. At least he knew Nolan's name thanks to their second round of exertions that morning.

"Oh, how lovely! Is this your piece then, Mr. Donovan? It's just charming."

"No, ma'm. Right now we are featuring the works of one of our up-and-coming artists. His name is Jasper, and I'd be happy to introduce him to you. As you can see, he's extremely talented. If you'll come with me, I'll take you to meet him and see more of his work." With that Nolan held out his hand for Skylar's mother.

Skylar trailed as Nolan held tight to his mother's hand and led her into the second gallery room. And then Skylar just gaped.

While the sculpture in the first room had been impressive, it was amazing to see this many creatures in this space. The room's tall ceilings and spacious layout easily housed the large sculptures. Colorful monsters and creatures with a hint of darkness were captured in whimsical and striking poses. It was like wandering into a garden of metal fantasy.

"Wow, these are amazing, Nolan," Skylar said as he looked around. "How did he ever come up with these?"

"Hey, Jasper, come on over here. These folks have questions on your pieces," Nolan called out, and almost immediately a nervous-looking young man approached. In the garden of colorful monsters, he was a fey creature, all sharp-edged feral beauty that could disappear at any second.

"Hi, I'm Jasper. I hope you are enjoying the show." Jasper looked around him with a fond smile for his creations, then returned his gaze to Skylar, biting his lip.

"Oh, hon, these are wonderful. When did you start making these?" Skylar's mom gushed at Jasper.

"A few years ago. I came across some stuff in a place I was staying. There were a lot of old industrial bits. And it kept reminding me of these creatures that were in my dreams as a kid. So I started putting the bits together. It didn't hold together very well, 'cause I didn't know really what I was doing, but I felt compelled to put it together," Jasper replied.

"And how did you learn to make them so intricate like this? These are just amazing, and your skill is impressive."

"I was trying to sell some small pieces down by the Castillo on the street, and Mr. Donovan saw them. He offered me a long-term contract with the gallery that included training, and that's been really helpful. Now that I really know how to weld and put things together, my creatures are so much closer to those in my imagination now. This past year he said they were perfect for the holiday show, so I worked hard on the ten pieces that are here."

Skylar noticed that Jasper got more confident as he continued to talk with his mother. He stepped back to give them some space and realized that Nolan had followed him. The two of them wandered out of earshot among the fantasy garden animals.

"I'm so sorry, Skylar. I didn't realize you were here with anyone. I never would have kissed you like that. I shouldn't have anyway, because I have no idea how you feel about PDA," Nolan said, with a sad face. "I hope I didn't ruin anything."

Skylar laughed. "It's okay. My mom knows very well that I'm gay, and PDAs are fine. I have nothing to hide. I just didn't expect you here, as I thought you had a date with your brothers tonight."

"We did, and we worked out our game plan over pizza. I really wanted to be here for the first night of Jasper's show, so I came as soon as I could."

They looked at each other, then Skylar began to chuckle. "Okay, so mutual awkwardness out of the way," he said to Nolan's quick grin.

"Your mom is amazing by the way. From what I can hear, she has Jasper entranced. Usually he's much more formal and reserved."

"How old is he anyway? He looks very young, but acts much older."

"He just turned twenty-one. He and I have been working together for about three years now. Since he's also a sculptor, I've had the pleasure of being able to personally mentor him, and I'm extremely proud of how well he's done. His natural talent is amazing."

"So is this a business or nonprofit? I'm a bit confused," Skylar asked, looking around at the beautiful space.

"Oh, it's a business. But... I inherited the gallery from my paternal grandmother. She had a fairly traditional selection of art when she was running it, but was always supporting local artists in other ways. I just kinda took that idea and expanded it. There's studio space and apartments around back, because sometimes people need a safe place to live and work to truly flourish. When the artists reach a point where the work they do is selected to be shown, they get the normal gallery rates and learn the business side too," Nolan said.

"Makes sense. And these pieces are amazing. But this one really calls to me. It reminds me of a ninja hippopotamus," Skylar said, stopping in front of a loudly purple creature that was captured in a leaping pose. "I think I may have to get it for the gym."

Nolan just laughed. "A ninja hippopotamus? Oh, Jasper will love that. And yeah, it would be perfect for a space like that. But are you sure? There's no obligation to buy anything, you know. Jasper's show will do well, and I am confident that his pieces will sell quickly."

"Of course I'm sure! Don't you dare sell it to anyone else. I want that hippo!" Skylar laughed as they walked back to his mother and the artist, who were chatting animatedly.

"I love seeing him so comfortable. This show is a major step in his career, and he's been extremely nervous. Heck, I've been nervous for him. But it's wonderful to see him put himself out there as an artist," Nolan said in an excited whisper as they drew closer, then raised his voice. "Hey, Jasper, Sky here wants your ninja hippo."

Nolan

"My hippo? Really?" Jasper whispered, looking shocked.

"You better believe it. We'll just put a sold sign up on it for tonight," Nolan said, then turned to Skylar. "Would it be okay if we leave it as part of the collection until after the holiday?"

"Yeah, that's fine. I will need to arrange to have it put in place properly in the gym. I assume that's something you can help me with?" Skylar asked, looking archly at Nolan.

"Yes, indeed. That will take a little time anyway, so I'm glad we can continue to show the piece. We'll set something up, most likely at the end of January."

Jasper just stood there looking slightly stunned until Nolan caught him up in a hug. "Congratulations. I told you that you'd sell pieces during the holiday show. This is just the first of many."

"Oh, it's so exciting! A new artist! I'm so glad we came in tonight," Skylar's mother enthused, reaching over to hug Jasper as well, who looked at her with a shy smile. Nolan just closed his eyes and breathed in, letting the happiness wash over him. This was exactly what he was in business to do. Why he had taken over the gallery and put so much time and effort into it. While he loved when every new artist had that first success, it was just a little more special with Jasper. The young man had such raw talent, and the determination to learn his craft.

"I'm glad you were here as well. Jasper is a talented artist, and everyone here is so proud of him," Nolan said.

"Of course. Now come, Jasper, can you show me the rest of your pieces? I'd love to hear what inspired you for these wonderful creations."

As Jasper wandered off, speaking excitedly to Skylar's mother, Nolan smiled. "Your mom is so sweet. And she's amazing at drawing him out of his shell."

"Yeah, she has a lot of experience working with young artists. She worked for 789 Dance for five years. They cut back on staff just last year, so I know she's loving the opportunity to talk with Jasper."

"Really? What kinds of things did she do there?"

"She worked there as a life skills coach. A lot of what she did was basic mentoring and encouragement. She worked as a real estate agent the entire time I was growing up and had a really successful career, so she could support me in my schooling and the time I took with training. But her educational background was in counseling. After I started the studio she retired from real estate and took up the part-time job that she always wanted. Unfortunately, that experience ended badly."

"Look, I'll be up-front and say while this is a business, obviously a large part of what I am trying to do is provide a strong foundation for young artists. I can pick talent, provide them with professional training and mentorship, but I don't have the time or ability to really provide them with all the skills they need to succeed in this field. Do you think your mom would be interested in a part-time job here?"

Skylar looked at Nolan, eyes wide. "Seriously? You would be willing to hire her to do that? Don't you need more time to think about it?"

"This is what I do, Skylar. I sign artists on the streets because of the talent that I see. It's the same with this. I'll need to talk to her about it after the holiday rush, but I think it makes sense for me to hire a part-time life coach for my artists. Some of them haven't had great role models, and need to learn some basic life skills like banking and finance. Others need help learning how to market both themselves and their art. It will help me out a great deal, since it frees me up from things I'm really not all that good at."

"Wow. I think she'd really like that," Skylar told him with a huge smile. "You'll have to ask her of course, but it sounds right up her alley."

"And speaking of things I'm not so good at…."

"Do I need to ask my mom to come over?" Skylar asked him, eyebrows arched.

Nolan laughed. "Oh God, no. I wanted to ask you a favor actually."

"A favor? Does it involve your luscious cock?"

Nolan felt his face turn beet red. "Um, well, actually, you see, I need a date. But it's for an awful family thing, and I don't want you to go in thinking it's just a simple date because it's… complicated. But yeah, I need a date and I was hoping you would be willing to help me out."

Skylar reached out and grabbed his shoulders as Nolan stood there stammering. "So why is it complicated?"

"My baby brother has asked his boyfriend to the big family Christmas event. His father, my stepfather, took it as well as I expected. That's why I never brought a date to one of those, because I didn't want to give him an excuse to cut me off from my brothers. But of course, now that Den has stepped up, you better believe that I'm going to support him. So all three of us are coming with male dates. Tor's isn't really a date, just his best friend, but the two girlfriends are plotting and planning and the whole thing is turning into a production. But yeah, I need a date. And you… well, you were who I thought of."

Skylar just stared at him. "Wow. Okay, that was a lot. But to sum up, you need a date for a super awkward family holiday event."

"Right. And right now I'm kinda obsessed with the idea of dressing you up and showing you off to the world. Make no mistake with the dress code, the idea is for us to shine and sparkle and be gay as fuck, to take some of the attention off my little brother."

"I'll have you know I can rock a tux. I happen to have one that's tailored to perfection to make me look fabulous. So how bad is this formal event likely to be?" Skylar asked.

"Well, the 1950s want my mom and stepfather back," Nolan said, and Skylar burst out laughing. "No, really. I love my mom, but I realized a long time ago that I never came first for her. She adored my father, and when he died she just broke. Then when she remarried, it was as if she got her mojo back. She's all tied up with being the perfect wife. And my stepfather is very rigid and the perfect embodiment of the 1950s company man. He has expectations of his family, most of which revolve around how they can support him in his career."

"That sounds kinda awful," Skylar murmured, reaching over to grasp Nolan's hand.

"I've always kept my personal life quiet, but that all changes now. So I need a date. In this case, I am offering up a full night of my luscious cock at your disposal if you will come along and play the part of doting boyfriend in my big fat gay coming out."

"Can I get a preview of coming attractions?" Skylar asked.

Without another word, Nolan grabbed his hand and dragged him back to his office. Skylar's mom had Jasper entranced, and Lisa was perfectly capable of managing the gallery. He had just stopped in to support Jasper on the first night of his show. And what a night it was turning out to be.

He swiftly closed the door and rounded on Skylar, stalking toward his prey. Skylar's eyes grew wide as Nolan stepped up and traced his cheekbones while he drew in his scent. Nolan moved his hands farther down the man's body until he reached his pants, and then he undid the zipper and drew out Skylar's cock.

"Commando. Nice. Makes this so much easier," Nolan said, then sank to his knees in front of Skylar. The whimpering above him was very nice and grew needy and desperate when Nolan licked the tip of Skylar's cock before he swallowed it down. He explored further and found Skylar's balls and caressed those with his hands while he did wicked things with his tongue to the cock that filled his mouth.

"I'm gonna, too much, Nolan!" came the incoherent cry above him as Skylar's balls drew up and a flood of cum filled his mouth. He swallowed happily, continuing to stroke his balls in a soothing motion. Skylar slumped heavily, leaning his hands on Nolan's shoulders.

"Wow," he breathed out. "Okay, deal. I'll come to the 50s revival party with you and shine like a beacon of gayness to the world."

Nolan laughed as he stood, pressing a kiss on Skylar's lips, letting the taste of the man's release linger on their mouths. Eventually, he pulled back just a bit as he tucked that beautiful cock back in, then rested his forehead against Skylar's. He just breathed and wondered at the feeling of contentment that shot through him at that moment.

"And consider that whole boyfriend thing?" he asked.

Skylar looked at him intently. "Is that really what you want?"

"Yes. I know it's sudden, but yes," Nolan said, struggling to explain. Words failing him, he pressed another kiss to Skylar's mouth. Until loud voices drifted in from the room outside.

"I'm sure he's probably in his office. Why he snuck back there rather than being out here dealing with all these people touring the gallery, I have no idea," Tor said from right outside.

"Remember, you just bought a hippo," Nolan said urgently, guiding Skylar into the nearest chair and walking behind his desk when the door opened. Damn. He really needed to remember to lock that thing.

"There you are! What are you doing hiding back here? Oh, sorry, I didn't realize someone was with you."

"Hey, Tor. This is Skylar. He owns Fortress Dojo, that fitness and karate studio over on Old St. Augustine. Most importantly, he bought one of Jasper's pieces, and we were making arrangements for delivery," Nolan said, trying to sound normal. "Skylar, this is my brother Tor. And this is Tor's best friend since forever, Byron."

Skylar shook both men's hands, and it was amusing to see him stand next to the two much taller young men. But Nolan knew just how much muscle and tone was hiding under Skylar's clothes… but no. He couldn't go down that path or he'd be useless to talk to anyone tonight. The drooling would get in the way.

"We left the rest of them out with your new featured artist."

"Well, let's go join them," Nolan said, leading the group out of his office with a sigh of relief. No one suspected a thing.

As they walked, Byron and Skylar discussed fitness routines and he fell in step with Tor, who promptly clasped his shoulder and whispered in his ear, "Dude, that fooled no one. Making arrangements? Those must be some sexy arrangements you work out with your clients."

"Tor!" Nolan managed to choke out just as they entered the showroom floor.

"Ah, there you two are!" Mrs. Lopez said as she caught sight of them. "I was just chatting with this charming young man here while Jasper gave the ladies a tour."

Nolan introduced everyone as Jasper returned with Julia and Jazz.

"It looks amazing, Jasper," Den said. "Nolan told us it was your opening night, so we just had to drop by."

"Thanks! It's been so exciting. I was really worried, but it's been, just, everything. Nolan, thank you. So much. This is beyond anything I could have imagined."

"That's my job, Jasper. Everyone is loving your pieces, as well they should," Nolan said firmly. "By the way, guys, Sky here has agreed to come with me to the holiday party. So please be nice to him. I don't want to give him the excuse to flee."

"That's a lot of arrangements for you to make, brother. Was there payment involved—Hey!" Tor yelled as Byron elbowed him.

"I'm glad you can come, Sky. I won't promise it will be fun, but it should be eventful," Den said. Nolan was struck again at how mature his little brother had become.

Skylar just laughed. "So I gather. And I will be honored to go with you and support you."

Nolan reached out a finger and traced it over Skylar's shimmering curls. "I thought you were coming with me, Shimmer."

"Awww," all three women breathed behind him.

I FEEL PRETTY

Skylar

Skylar could not believe he was doing this. Really. Nolan had warned him, but no, he hadn't taken him seriously. And now... he was about to join Nolan's brothers and their dates at a spa for treatments with all of Jazz's apparently copious aunts there to supervise. And Nolan, who was going to be a bit late because of a last-minute "art emergency." Damn that man.

Taking a deep breath, he entered the upscale spa, pausing in the entrance as he allowed the calming wood-plank decor and barely heard music to soothe him.

"Skylar!" said a voice off to the side. Then a sudden missile launched at him and right into his side. All sense of calm promptly fled.

"Julia, sweet, I said I would come." He had to admit he had been surprised when Julia had called him in the middle of the week to suggest the spa day, but there was no way he was going to refuse the invitation. He had really enjoyed meeting Nolan's brothers and friends and was looking forward to spending more time with them.

"I know, I know. I'm just excited! This will be so much fun," she exclaimed, grabbing his hand and dragging him through the lobby.

As he entered the room that had been set aside for them, Den sat front and center looking miserable, and he burst out laughing.

"Is it truly that bad, Den?" he asked.

"Look around, man. So much…," Den muttered under his breath. "Tor and Byron are just basking in all the attention."

Skylar had to laugh because Den was right. The two men were at the center of *a lot* of female attention as they got primped to within an inch of their lives. And they were quite literally preening as they sat shirtless with the women slathering mud masks on their faces.

"Skylar, this is my boyfriend, Aaron. Who I think is raking in the points owed for every minute we are here," Den said, introducing the absolute cutie standing next to him. He had a mop of luscious curls that framed a dark-skinned cherubic face and hazel eyes.

"Thanks so much, Jazz! I can't believe your aunt Cathy owns this place. It's so sweet of her and her sisters to host us!" Julia exclaimed.

"Well, we did promise her hot pictures of Tor and Byron in return," Jazz reminded her friend. "Speaking of which, time for a pic, guys!"

The two friends just laughed and happily posed together. It looked absurd, especially when they started to make ridiculous faces that cracked the mud. The girls who were hovering seemed happy with the pose as well. Come to think of it, Skylar thought as he contemplated the abs on display, maybe it wasn't all that ridiculous.

"Hey, no perving on the straight guys," Nolan said as he wrapped Skylar up in a hug. "Especially not the straight guy that's my little brother."

Skylar just laughed. "No worries, darling. Just trying to figure out if that pose was ridiculously hot or just ridiculous, and I'm really not sure."

"I suspect that Julia and Jazz would tell you their boyfriends are ridiculously hot. Personally, I think the green stuff on their face just doesn't offset their hair very well." Nolan shrugged and grabbed Skylar's hand. "Let's go rescue the youngsters and get them somewhere less… overwhelming."

After collecting Den and Aaron, they headed over to several stations in a quiet corner of the room. Two of the aunts came over and assessed them critically.

"Okay, darlings, my name is Ira and this is Lydia. I see you have fled the scene. But we shall still get you all ready for the big night. Ms. Wayfair was most adamant that you gentlemen will look marvelous when leaving here. Let's start with something easy, shall we, and soak your hands and feet? I promise you won't melt or anything. It will merely feel wonderful, especially with a bit of massage."

The two women quickly set up seats with appropriate places to soak, and Skylar settled back with a sigh and allowed the deliciously warm water and smell of mint to do its magic. Ira and Lydia worked quietly, and soon enough they had been soaked and scrubbed and massaged, finally ending with a facial and head massage.

Suddenly a burst of laughter erupted from Den. "Aaron, love, your hair is ridiculous right now."

Sure enough, Aaron's curls had morphed into a raging case of bedhead with a side of static electricity.

"Good thing we have the stylist right here to finish up," Ira said, waving over a young man who had just arrived. Thankfully it didn't take too much longer, and Skylar knew his color was still perfection, so a quick trim and he was ready to go. He looked around, and damn, did they clean up nice. Den and Aaron definitely looked the most changed, and he smiled at the transformation.

"Don't you look good!" Julia said as she came over and gave Den a kiss on the cheek. "Not too painful, was it, guys?"

Den just grumbled as the rest of them laughed.

Nolan

Nolan took stock of the havoc that had been wreaked in his house. Formal wear was strewn in bits and pieces all over his bedrooms. Julia and Jazz had taken over his kitchen and back deck to take pictures once everyone was ready. The bathrooms were saturated with styling products, and water had been splashed everywhere. But he grinned from ear to ear as he looked at his family and friends. Getting ready for the formal event tonight had taken on a life of its own, and they had their own pre-party going on. Sadly, Nolan suspected that this one was a lot more fun than the real party to come later.

Tor and Byron came out of the guest bedroom, followed closely by half of the basketball team. The other half were wandering through his living room, carrying beers and playing on the PS4. Loudly. But the noise died down as everyone got to see the final unveiling. Julia and Jazz rushed in and squealed.

They did look amazing. Tor wore a traditional tuxedo, which had been tailor-made for him, and a deep purple shirt. The outfit set off his mahogany hair and piercing blue eyes. Byron also had on a traditional tuxedo, but with a white shirt that highlighted his sculpted cheekbones and dark skin. He had always reminded Nolan a little bit of Denzel Washington. Tor and Byron together were a striking couple. The girls immediately grabbed them into the other room for a photo session, working their friends in on the fun as well.

Once the chaos had been removed to the kitchen, Den and Aaron hesitantly came out. They had gone for straight-up traditional. Den had cleaned up well, and it was amazing to see how dashing he looked now. Aaron...well, that boy was all kinds of adorable. Nolan could see why Den was so enamored.

Cordelia stepped up to help both young men with the finishing touches on their ties. She had insisted on coming over with Skylar to make sure the youngsters had someone looking out for them. From the way the two were smiling shyly at her, they were both basking in her attention. There was something about her that just shouted out "Mom" with all capital letters and cookies.

Nolan turned when Skylar came over, a water bottle held out. "Thanks, Shimmer. You look amazing."

And he did. The man was wearing a tuxedo that had a deep royal blue tint, and a peacock-style vest. The combination played off his amazing hair and made for quite the breathtaking sight. Nolan had chosen to wear his normal tuxedo, as it was tailored to perfection. But he'd paired it with a steel-blue shirt and a royal-blue bow tie. He was vain enough to hope it highlighted his deep blue eyes.

Cordelia hugged them both. "Look at you two! The six of you are going to make quite an entrance."

"Speaking of making an entrance, let's go face the music and let the girls take our pictures," Nolan told the group as he dragged everyone to the kitchen. When he got there, photos were being taken out on the deck. Julia and Jazz had put their boyfriends in the middle surrounded by the rest of the basketball team, who were all in uniform. He had no idea how the girls had talked them into that, but he suspected they could talk just about anyone into doing what they wanted. The Christmas lights he had strung along the railings shone brightly in the early evening light, providing a nice lighting backdrop for the pictures.

"These are great. The site is going to go through the roof again. The likes from the spa day were amazing, and this is going to be even better!" Jazz exclaimed excitedly.

Skylar took her phone and herded the two girls into the picture. A couple of the guys placed the girls on their shoulders behind their boyfriends. Nolan laughed when the team tossed around several basketballs covered in Santa hats. Nolan was seriously impressed that the entire team had taken everything in stride and were all here to support their teammates. Skylar took a bunch of photos and handed the phone back for the girls to sort through once they jumped down.

Nolan grabbed Skylar as they wandered back into the kitchen and kissed him hard, then realized that they had an audience who was doing their best paparazzi impression.

"So. Hot. OMG," Julia muttered, and he had to stifle his grin as he looked over at her.

"Jazz, I'm not sure it will be safe to post those pictures. Ovaries will explode." Julia chuckled.

"If we don't post that picture, the team will never forgive us. They agreed to stay home today as long as we posted enough pictures. Poor Nolan had enough people showing up at his house. Okay, we just need a picture of Den and Aaron, and then one of all of you," Jazz said, fully in control of the situation. The rest of the pictures went quickly, and then it was time to load up into the limo that Nolan had arranged for the evening. The rest of the guests in the house were planning to stick around until they came back.

"Call us if you need us to come down there and kick anyone's ass," Julia said. Nolan caught her up in a huge hug, glad that Tor had found someone so amazing to be by his side.

PARTY DOWN

Skylar

Skylar held tight to Nolan's hand as they approached the entrance to the building. He hadn't been too sure exactly what this "family holiday event" would look like, but apparently, it involved renting out the exclusive club at the private golf course. Much like downtown, there were lights everywhere, and the palm trees, in particular, were sparkling. Christmas music could be heard throughout the grounds, and the current song about a white Christmas was particularly out of place in the almost seventy-degree weather.

"You look like you are expecting the gators to pop up. You can relax—they live down on the 16th hole," Tor told him, slapping his shoulder.

"I suspect, looking at the crowd I see here, the gators may be more friendly," Skylar said wryly.

"Ha! You may be right," Den said, taking a deep breath.

"Den, you don't have to do this. We don't have to do this. Skylar, Byron, and I can go hit the diner for real food while you guys go schmooze with the relations. Don't force it if you aren't ready," Aaron said quietly.

"Aaron, hon, I am ready. You are everything to me, and I need them to know that. I don't mean to drop you into the gator frenzy that is about to erupt, but I really need you with me. This is for me, and it's for us. I... need you beside me everywhere, here included. Or I'm not me anymore," Den said, shaking his head in frustration. "I'm not explaining this well...."

"Shhh. I get it. I do. So let's go in there and be fearless," Aaron replied, holding tightly to Den's hand. The love and courage in the moment made Skylar's eyes water.

"Fearless!" Tor and Byron chanted in unison and chest bumped each other. Skylar burst out laughing, because, really. Such total jocks, even if they were a complete surprise in many ways. The support that they and the rest of their team had shown for Den today had blown him away. And they had managed to take him from tears to laughter in seconds. He suspected that tonight's emotional whiplash had just started.

"You guys are such dorks!" Den exclaimed, shaking his head. "But... you are the best brothers a guy could have. Thank you all for doing this with us."

"You do not need to thank us for supporting you. That's what we're here for, little brother. Come then," Nolan said, grabbing ahold of Skylar's arm and taking the lead as they approached the door.

"Yeah, come on, little brother," Byron said, chest puffed out as he ruffled Den's hair, then grabbed Tor's hand.

"Not the hair! And I already have two older brothers," Den protested as he laughed and grabbed Aaron's hand.

"I think you have three," Aaron said quietly, with a big smile on his face.

Skylar chuckled at the antics behind him, then it was show time as they were about to enter the club. Tonight was about Den and supporting him while he made a stand. This had become his fight, and he wouldn't let the younger man down.

With that in mind, bolstering his confidence, he held tight to Nolan's arm as they walked into the large room beyond. The party was in full swing, well, as exciting as it could get with everyone in formal wear and trying to look sophisticated. He felt the others enter behind him, and then an odd silence rippled around the room. Even without the "gay" thing going on, he suspected that the six of them entering together would catch everyone's attention.

"Mother! So good to see you. I hope Dad's here. We've been looking forward to seeing everyone. We even got Tor and Den all cleaned up and presentable. Don't they look great?" Nolan said in a bright, artificially cheerful voice as he steered them over to a woman standing near the door. She had a deer-in-the-headlights look about her as she watched them approach.

Nolan

He held tightly on to Skylar's hand as they walked up to his mother. She was frozen, glass in hand. Definitely not a welcoming look. He sighed, as it shouldn't have been a surprise. He had called her and told her of their plan to come tonight. She had freaked out and told him not to attend, but he had hoped his argument of needing to support her youngest son would resonate with her when she had a chance to reflect on it. He breathed a sigh of relief as he realized she was standing next to Mrs. Amwith, a longtime client at the gallery.

"Nolan! Dear, it's so good to see you. I was just telling your mother how much I enjoyed the latest piece I bought from you. That dragon painting just looks divine in my sitting room," she exclaimed.

"I'm so glad. You should stop in sometime during the holiday event. I have a new sculptor that has such marvelous creations. I think one would be perfect for your garden," he said as he kissed her cheek. "Mrs. Amwith, may I introduce you to my boyfriend Skylar?"

Skylar stepped up and took Mrs. Amwith's hand, turning it and pressing a kiss to her knuckles as she blushed in surprised delight. Definitely showtime.

"Oh, so handsome and sweet you are! I love your tux, darling. And your hair! Do you think I could pull that look off? I'm pretty sure it would look amazing. I think I should make you my fashion consultant!"

"Sadly, I am not as talented as all that. My friend Jared is a stylist in town and put together this ensemble for me when I needed formal wear," Skylar replied.

"Oh, what is it that you do, Skylar?" Mrs. Amwith asked. Nolan noted that his mother remained quiet, letting her friend handle the conversation. He wished he knew what she was thinking.

"I own Fortress Dojo, a fitness and karate studio in town. It keeps me busy, and I've joined a number of the business associations of course. Hence the need for the formal wear. Otherwise, I fear, my attire is entirely suited for being in a gym."

Or of course at a dance club, but Nolan kept that particular thought to himself. Before he got too distracted by remembering Skylar's attire the previous weekend, the rest of the group arrived, having diverted to pick up drinks along the way. Tor handed Nolan and Skylar each a glass, then reclaimed his own from Byron.

"Hello, Mrs. Novac. It's good to see you again," Byron said to Nolan's mother, reaching out his hand.

Still apparently in a daze, she took his hand automatically. "Um, hello, Byron. It is good to see you as well. Victor, where is Julia?"

"Oh, she couldn't make it tonight so Byron volunteered to keep me company. Isn't that great?" Tor said.

"Yes, well, great. I'm always glad to see your friends, Victor. And you, Riorden, you look very nice this evening," Nolan's mother continued, obviously still flustered.

"Thank you, Mother. I think you met Aaron last weekend when he came over for lunch," Den said dryly. "He was gracious enough to agree to come with me tonight."

Nolan stifled a laugh, and grasped hold of Skylar's hand.

"Oh my gosh, Victoria, is this little Riorden? You look so grown up! And is this your boyfriend?" Mrs. Amwith exclaimed excitedly, oblivious to the tension in the area. Or perhaps not so oblivious, as she turned to him and winked.

"Nice to meet you, ma'am. I'm Aaron. Aaron Seevers," he stammered out as he shook her hand.

Mrs. Amwith promptly pulled him into a hug, then held him at arm's length. "I can definitely see why Riorden is so enamored, yes? So very handsome you both are. Why I think you two are the same age as my nephews. They just came over this past weekend to help me decorate. I do declare, I've lived here for half my life, but it still seems wrong to decorate for Christmas while wearing shorts."

Nolan laughed. "Missing the snow from Pittsburgh, Mrs. Amwith?"

"No, I can't say I miss the snow and ice. But there's something to be said for the traditional Christmas decor with pine trees and a dusting of snow. Instead, I had my nephews sweating up a storm while they hung lights on my palm trees. Here, take a look," she said, handing Nolan her phone.

When he burst into laughter, Skylar looked over to see the screen. There was a large lawn with four impressive palm trees that were decked out in an eye-melting amount of lights. The bottoms were red lights that tapered up over the natural bulge in the tree, and then it switched to white lights as it cascaded up over the top of the fronds.

"That, um, that looks… ummm," Skylar burst out.

"Looks just like a bunch of dicks in the yard, doesn't it?" she said, as her frown twitched into light laughter. "My poor nephews are mortified as they thought I would switch out the lights, but I left them just like they are and pretend I have no idea what they look like and show them off to everyone. Very loudly if they happen to be around, and credit them with how well the decorations turned out. I must say, there are times when I love Christmas in Florida."

Just then Nolan's stepfather approached them, drink in hand and scowl on his face.

"Jules! I was just getting reacquainted with your lovely family. Such handsome and well-mannered young men. And they definitely do you proud with their attire this evening. And their dates are just enchanting!" Mrs. Amwith gushed.

"So very nice of you to say, Lucy," Jules Novac said, settling his stare on Nolan and glaring. "If you will excuse me, I need to borrow Nolan for a second."

With that he turned and stalked away, obviously expecting Nolan to follow him.

"Pardon me for just a moment. I'll be back as soon as I can," Nolan said, squeezing Skylar's hand as he whispered in his ear, "Please make sure to keep Den here, no matter what."

"So tell me, Skylar, what type of classes do you offer?" Mrs. Amwith asked as he followed after his stepfather. He smiled to realize that he had left the group in excellent hands.

They reached the french doors and went out onto the patio. The evening was extremely pleasant, and the lights twinkled in the back of the club area as well. In addition to the lights on the building, there was a truly impressive display of Christmas lights on the trees and shrubbery. Including the palm trees, but these were much more sedately decorated than Mrs. Amwith's display. It would be a relaxing view, except for the man that rounded on him as soon as he stepped outside.

"What the ever-loving fuck do you think you and your brothers are trying to do? I forbade Riorden from bringing that boy with him tonight. And what the hell is Victor thinking to bring that obnoxious friend of his along? And you? You've always had the sense to be discreet. I expect that you will respect my wishes and send the three stooges that you lot came with home right away."

Nolan struggled with how best to reply and finally settled on the straightforward approach. "No."

"What do you mean no? That's not acceptable, Nolan. Your brother was told already what the implications of disobedience would be. I cannot allow you to flaunt your disrespect in front of my friends and business associates!"

"No disrespect was intended, sir. All we did was attend the party with our dates. If you are determined in this, all six of us can leave now. Before dinner. But be warned that if we do that, we will not be coming back. Den will stay with Tor and me. I repeat, we will not be back."

"Nolan! No! You can't do that. Did you talk your brothers into this? Why must you make this so difficult?" his mother exclaimed as she walked up to them.

"Why hello, Mother. So glad to see your never-ending love and support—"

His stepfather slapped him across the face.

"You will not disrespect your mother or me like that!" he shouted, as Nolan deliberately caressed the red spot on his cheek.

He sighed as Tor and Byron stepped up to flank him. He was glad that the rest of the group hadn't arrived yet. Hopefully, Skylar and Mrs. Amwith could keep the boys distracted.

"There is no disrespect intended. But Riorden told you what he wanted, no, what he needed from you. Telling him to stay in the closet is not an appropriate answer. I stayed discreet, yes, but that was so that you could not cut me off from my brothers. So now I must do what I need to protect them, as I always have."

"Nolan, I…," Tor began, then stopped after his father turned to glare at him.

"You will do nothing! You will walk out of here, with the rest of this lot, and leave Riorden to us. He will learn to respect the rules we have laid down for him."

"Sorry, but no. I have seen what type of learning that is. Unfortunately for you, I have records of it as well. From Christmas of ten years ago in fact. If you want to turn this into a fight that will get all sorts of press, I can petition for custody out of concern for Riorden's safety. The video I have will make for interesting evidence."

His mother gasped as his stepfather blanched.

"What video? What are you talking about, Nolan?" his mother asked, looking panicked.

"The one I made using the motion-triggered camera you had given me for my birthday one year. It was right before I moved out. When I moved in with Grandma and started working at the gallery," he replied carefully.

"But I thought you said you were moving out to give us more room for Riorden and Victor, and because Grandma needed help."

Nolan laughed bitterly. "Both those things were true. But I also realized I wasn't welcome in his house," he said, nodding at his stepfather. Then suddenly he had a terrible thought and tears welled in his eyes. "I thought Tor and Den would be safe. He didn't hurt you, did he, Tor? Please tell me he didn't hurt you."

Tor rushed over to grab his arm. "No, he never touched me. By the time you moved out, I was already bigger than you. And I was always doing everything he wanted anyway, between school and sports. So no, I was safe. He didn't mess with Den either, not until last weekend when I grabbed him. Don't cry, Nolan. You aren't responsible for any of this."

Nolan took a deep breath and addressed his mother. "I have the video on my phone if you don't believe me. The one where he beat me and told me I couldn't date boys and be part of his family. Where he threatened to cut me off from all contact with my brothers if I didn't change my ways."

"I… I don't know what's come over you. All of you! But I won't put up with being humiliated. Take your brothers and your ridiculous dates and get out of here. I don't care what you do with the little pervert, but keep him away from me," Nolan's stepfather said, glaring at him and Tor. "And don't you dare let anyone else see that video or I'll call in some favors, and maybe that gallery of yours won't do so well…."

"What the…." Tor began, rushing at his father, but Nolan grabbed his arm. "No, Tor. Let's just walk away. We don't mess with him, and he won't mess with us. Agreed?"

"Goddamn you, yes. Just get out of my sight. I don't want you coming to me for anything, you hear me? As for Riorden, well, good luck with him. My lawyer will be in touch to finalize guardianship papers. Come, Victoria, we are done here."

And his mother walked off with her husband without a backward glance.

PAYBACKS

Skylar

"I think you owe me something, and I believe it was supposed to be exquisite," he said, looking at Nolan as they got into the limo. His date had come back with his brother and Byron, all three looking furious but trying to contain it. Skylar was more concerned with the red welt that had appeared on Nolan's cheek while they were gone. They had made their excuses to Mrs. Amwith, and Nolan had bundled everyone outside.

"Do I now?" Nolan asked, but with a flash of a smile that made Skylar take a relieved breath. The look on Nolan's face when they first reached the limo had been devastating and he had been desperate to distract him.

"Hey, no sex in the limo. That's just wrong. There are things I don't need to know about my big brother," said Tor, getting in after them with Byron by his side.

"Move over, guys. Dang, you two are blocking the door with your big butts. I swear we brought the entire basketball team with us rather than just the two of you based on all that real estate," came Den's complaining voice. Skylar smiled at the thought that the boy could complain like a typical teen after this, knowing he had the love and support of his brothers. It wasn't going to be all rainbow unicorns and it didn't seem like a family reunion was in the works. But Den would have the full support of his brothers and their friends, and the road in front of him wouldn't be a lonely one filled with jagged secrets.

While Skylar envied Den the camaraderie that came with his brothers and their extended circle, he was once again grateful for the amazing advocate his mother had been while he was growing up. Her strength and belief in him had kept him going on many difficult days, and he had to smile at her fierceness.

"I love seeing that smile on your face," Nolan said quietly as he squeezed his hand, then turned to the rest of the group. "We're all going back to my house so we can let the girls collect the conquering horde and whisk you all and your grooming supplies back to the apartment. The limo will wait for you and the girls while you get your stuff."

"Hey, Tor, are you sure it's okay if I crash with you again tonight?" Den asked.

"Of course, little bro. The couch is all yours for the holidays. I really like the idea of hanging out with you for a few weeks. That will give Nolan some alone time tonight," Tor said, with a wink for his older brother.

"Is it okay if I stay over tonight too? My folks know where I went and I told them I would be back tomorrow. I didn't want to make them wait up," Aaron asked tentatively.

"No problem. I'll actually be going over to Jazz's place tonight. So feel free to crash in my room," Byron said.

"Awesome! Thanks, Byron," said Den.

"Just no sex in my bed. Hard limit, man. You're my little brother, and that would just be all wrong," Byron hastily put in.

"You two are all full of no-fun rules," Skylar said laughingly. "No sex in the limo, no sex in the bed. I guess that leaves wall sex? I can be down with that."

Once they reached Nolan's house, they all piled out and headed in, and Skylar made coffee while the rest of them gathered their stuff. Julia and Jazz joined him in the kitchen while he was working. It looked like the two of them had been busy fixing the chaos that had been left. And of course lighting up social media.

"Um, so how did it go?" Julia asked softly.

"I am going to go out on a limb and say badly. We had a wonderful chat with a Mrs. Amwith, but then the evil stepfather took Nolan out for a chat. Let's just say we departed shortly thereafter."

"That's a good summary, pretty boy." Tor walked into the kitchen with the rest of the crew and pulled Julia in for a kiss. "Den is coming back with us tonight, and Aaron is going to have a sleepover I think. Right, guys?" he asked his younger brother and his date.

"We didn't really talk about anything, but I guess I'm not going home?"

Nolan grabbed his youngest brother up in his arms. "No, Den. You won't be going home. I didn't want to make any decisions for you and hoped we could avoid that. But things didn't work out like I hoped."

"Did he hit you? Is that why your cheek is red?"

"Yes, and that's why I don't want you going home. I never want you there by yourself, okay? Did he hit you before?"

"No, but he got all sorts of mad the day I left. That's why Tor grabbed me. I think he really wanted to hit me, and it freaked me out," Riorden said softly as Aaron hugged him tightly.

"It will be all right, Den. You have us. We'll never turn our backs on you," Nolan said fiercely.

"And us! You have us! And a whole bunch of my family thinks you are all sorts of adorable. A few of them wanted to keep you after the spa day. So if you ever need rides or anything and your brothers aren't around, you just give us a call," Jazz said. Her eyes were brimming with tears, but she sounded excited at the same time.

"I want you to always make decisions for yourself, Den. I know it's hard to feel forced into things because you aren't old enough to be on your own yet. Believe me, I know. But for right now, the plan is for you to stay with Tor for the holiday. Things will be a bit hectic once school starts back up again for both of you, so I'd like you to come stay with me then. This house is plenty big, and we'll set up the guest room for you, okay? We'll get everything straightened out with the school in the meantime."

"Yeah, that sounds good. I... thank you—"

Nolan cut him off with a huge hug. "Never thank me for loving you, brother. We're a family, and we're going to stick together," Nolan said roughly.

"Hey, I'm pretty sure Dad was going to get me a sweet ride for Christmas this year. Since you're taking over the role, does that mean you'll take me car shopping this week?" Den asked brightly.

"In your dreams, smartass," Nolan replied, ridiculously happy with his brother's resilient spirit. "Now you guys get out of here. It's late, and I think we all need our rest."

"If that's what you're going with, bro," Tor muttered, before Julia grabbed his arm and dragged him out, the rest of them following and laughing.

Nolan

"Well, that was about as bad as it could possibly go," Nolan said as he sank down on the seat after the door closed.

"What happened with your folks?" Skylar asked quietly.

"Oh, Den's father tried to kick us all out but have us leave Den there. Since things had gone south before Tor rescued him last week, I didn't feel it was safe to leave him, Sky. So I had to resort to blackmail."

"Blackmail?" Skylar asked.

"I have a video of him beating me the night he threw me out ten years ago before I went and lived with my grandmother. I haven't used it before, but I'm glad I kept it as a just-in-case."

"And your face? Did he hit you again?" Skylar asked, running his finger tenderly down the side of Nolan's face where he could still feel the impact of his stepfather's hand.

"Yeah, he was really angry," Nolan said, startled by the flash of anger on Skylar's face.

"Shit. I should have gone with you. Mrs. Amwith was fine with the boys. Never again. He doesn't ever get to lay a hand on you again," Skylar said, staring intently at Nolan.

"I'm fine. Really. I'm more upset by my mother's reaction tonight than anything else."

"What about your mom?" Skylar asked.

Nolan smiled bitterly. "She didn't say anything really. Just insisted how wrong I was. But she left with her husband when he stormed off. I mean, it's not like I didn't know he was the most important thing to her. But I had hoped that she would step up and truly be a mother for Den and love him unconditionally. I had really wanted that for him, which is why we went to that stupid party tonight. What a waste."

"Oh, hon, it was many things but not a waste. While it may not be the answer you wanted, you now know what the plan is for your brother. And he'll be loved and protected. And my mother is going to be all over that boy. He won't know what hit him," Skylar said with a wink. "And besides, it got you all dressed up in this tux, which has made me hard all night. It's a good thing we didn't stick around for dancing. I don't think I could've moved without pain."

Nolan laughed, feeling suddenly light-hearted, and grabbed Skylar up in his arms. "I don't know how you do it, but with you, I feel like it will actually be all right."

"Of course it will, once you get to work on my reward. Remember the one I get for coming tonight?"

"Oh, you'll be coming tonight. Let's just see how many times we can make that happen." And with that Nolan crushed his mouth down on Skylar's, feasting ravenously on his lips. He gave thanks for the fact that all the blinds had been closed and languidly began to undress the beautiful man in front of him. He bent down to untie his shoes and help him out of his footwear before moving on to the rest of his clothes. He carefully placed the amazing outfit on a nearby chair, then lifted Skylar up onto the table. He gave further thanks for his obvious foresight in furniture selection, the piece being an artistic masterpiece in wood and stone that had been bolted to the floor. It was beautiful and extremely sturdy.

He leaned over and stared down at Skylar, basking in the sight of his lover beneath him, as contentment snuck into his heart.

"Nolan? Is this okay? We don't have to if you need time to…. I mean, I was only kidding about the payback and you don't—"

Nolan took his cock in his mouth and sucked for all he was worth. Inarticulate cries were wrung from Skylar's lips as Nolan focused all of his attention on this one moment, on this one man.

He reached into the inside pocket of his tuxedo and drew out the supplies he had stashed there. He placed the foil packet down and quickly opened the lube. With slicked fingers, he gently probed Skylar's entrance, and his finger was drawn into the welcoming heat. The cries grew louder and more desperate until he had three fingers in his lover's channel and that beautiful cock deep down his throat, and then there were only whimpers.

"Stop, please, I want to come with you filling me up. Please, Nolan, I need you inside me...."

He withdrew his fingers and shucked his pants, drawing out his cock. He stood up and slipped on the condom, then slicked himself up quickly. He positioned himself and thrust deep, knowing Skylar relished the entry and burn. He stopped once he was balls deep and slowly stroked Skylar's cock.

"You gonna start moving there, bad boy?"

"Bossy bottom." Nolan laughed as he glided in and out in a teasing rhythm.

"Move, damn you, move!" Skylar demanded as he reached up and twisted ever so slightly on Nolan's piercing. Damn. That felt amazing. Giving over entirely to the sensations, he thrust over and over until he was almost at the edge and then plunged right over it when Skylar cried out his release and his channel spasmed in rhythm with his orgasm.

"Okay, so it was table sex rather than wall sex. Still works," muttered the man sprawled out all over said piece of furniture. Nolan laughed as he carefully withdrew, grabbing a towel that lay nearby and cleaned them up before carefully covering his lover's body with his own, propped up on his arms so he could admire the man beneath him.

"Only one problem. The bed is all the way over there. I'm not sure I can make it. I think you wrecked me."

"Hon, if I had truly wrecked you, you wouldn't be able to talk right now. We'll have to work on that. In the meantime...." With that Skylar levered himself up, somehow taking Nolan with him and lifting him over his shoulder before carrying him into the bedroom and throwing him onto his bed.

"Dang tricky ninja."

"Hey, I have a ninja hippo to try to live up to now. I need to step up the training, I think."

"You can train on me anytime."

"I stepped right into that one, didn't I?" He smiled down at Nolan. "You're still wearing most of your clothes, including your shoes. It's kinda cute, but not exactly comfortable for bed. Let's get you undressed."

As Skylar reached for him, Nolan caught his hand, bringing it to his lips.

"Stay," he ordered. "Stay the night."

"I had planned to, remember? I have my overnight bag stashed in here already." Skylar smiled at him fondly.

"Fair warning, I want lots of overnights. And eventually, I want the bag to be unnecessary. I want us to wake up Christmas morning together. And kiss on New Year's Eve. You're mine. I knew that from the moment I saw you in my bed that first morning, when you enchanted me beyond reason."

Skylar was quiet for a long moment. "And do I get to keep you too?"

"Always. Always yours, Shimmer. Please never let me go."

"Never. Always yours," Skylar said as he carefully helped Nolan undress. Nolan drew the smaller man into his arms and closed his eyes, happiness washing through him in endless bounds.

"Love you, Shimmer. Always you."

RAINBOWS IN SEA GLASS

Kyle has loved James, his best friend's older brother, for as long as he can remember. Unfortunately, James is a player, and Kyle has no desire to be his latest conquest. When James suddenly turns the full weight of his charm on him, Kyle flees to Cape May Point to collect sea glass and Cape May diamonds to make a St. Nicholas Day present for his aunt.

James has always taken Kyle's presence for granted and he's shocked to find how integral Kyle is to his life and future happiness. Braving his family's well-meaning attempts to help and a sudden winter storm, James heads to the shore to convince Kyle that the most precious thing they'll find on the beach is each other.

CHAPTER 1

Kyle

"GET THE fuck out," Kyle said, his brain scattered on the four winds. Or was it five? He could never remember.

"No, really. I think he's perfect for you," Maria insisted as she spun around to stop him from leaving.

"Maria. I'm not falling for this one." Kyle sidestepped her and kept walking. "The last guy you thought was perfect for me talked about 401(k) all night. I still have nightmares about compounding interest rates."

"Okay, fine. I just get concerned. You've been really quiet lately and not coming out with us," Maria said as she rushed past to get to the door of the diner.

"I've just been busy. You know that. Things are really taking off with my design clients right now. We roll out that new website next week." All true. Every last word.

Kyle was happy to see Tom waiting for them by the door. The diner owner waved them over to their normal Sunday morning booth and brought coffee over.

"You two getting the usual?" Tom asked. His ugly sweater had a Christmas tree on it with actual light-up decorations that flashed in a cheerful pattern.

"Yeah, and keep the coffee coming," Maria said.

"Late night?" Tom asked with a smirk. "Seems like pretty boy has you beat—he looks all fresh and rested."

"Kyle has turned into a pod creature who doesn't want to spend time with his friends at night," Maria said tartly as Tom started to laugh. The man had a booming laugh that was infectious. He had to be in his sixties now, and he and his wife had owned this place as long as anyone could remember.

"I'll go get your order in. You two behave yourselves, and don't scare off the rest of the clientele," Tom admonished as he walked away.

"Hey, it was only the one time!" Maria called after him with a pout.

The place had the usual crowd for a Sunday morning. There were only a few tables occupied due to the early hour. To the left was a large table packed with college kids who had obviously not gotten home yet after a rough night out. Over by the window was a table with four guys in leathers who were all set to go on a nice Sunday ride. Their bikes were right outside, and he drooled a bit at all that chrome.

One of the guys was the very picture of "leather daddy," and Kyle couldn't help but appreciate the view. Just as he was indulging himself checking out the eye candy, biker dude looked up and winked at him. Kyle flushed bright red before turning back to Maria.

"Oh my God. You totally got caught. I can't believe you got caught," Maria breathed out. "That was classic."

"Hey, can you blame me? Really?"

"Okay, point." She glanced over at the table herself and cringed when the four guys saluted her and started to laugh. "And luckily the biker dudes think we are hysterical. I doubt Tom wants to break up a fight at his diner on a Sunday morning."

"That wouldn't be a fight," Tom said as he brought over the muffins. "It would be a mauling. Nah, those guys are cool. And I think you've given them a story to bring home to their wives tonight."

"Married?" Maria asked, disappointment in her voice.

"Would you stop trying to set me up with everyone you see?" Though to be honest, biker dude didn't look like he'd be a boring date.

"Hey, not everything is about you, sweetie. I wouldn't mind a ride on his bike as it were," Maria replied pertly.

"You did not just say that," Kyle told her as Tom walked away laughing again.

"I've missed you," Maria said, laughter gone from her voice.

"How is that even possible? You text me at least twenty times a day, and we get together…."

"No, Kyle Miller, we don't. We do brunch once a week. But Saturday night used to be our thing. I could count on you to make me laugh and make me look awesome on the dance floor. Everyone has been asking about you. James was on my case last night asking where you were. Everything was just great, and then six months ago you go poof."

"I have not gone poof. I'm right here in front of you. See?" Kyle bounced his hand up and down on her dark red curls. "These, on the other hand, went poof sometime last night. Your hair needs some serious repair, sweetheart."

"Don't deflect! What's the deal?"

"I told you, life's been busy. Now let's eat." Kyle thanked every deity under the sun that Tom arrived just then with the food. Because Maria was right—he had been ghosting everyone. But six months ago, when they had all been out at the club, James had actually danced with him, seduction in every movement. It was a startling change from the fond amusement that normally tinged his interactions with James. The lifelong infatuation Kyle had for his best friend's older brother had gone straight to Mayday territory.

The thought of becoming yet another person in James's bed was a nightmare straight from hell. James had always been there for him and his sister Maria, and there was no doubt that he loved them both. Sadly, Kyle knew his own limitations, and there was no way he could stay away from James now that he had shown the tiniest iota of interest. Kyle had no willpower when it came to the star of almost every one of his fantasies. He had hidden himself away from temptation packaged in six feet of well-toned ginger goodness.

"I'll let you off this time," Maria said as she dug into her pancakes and sighed with contentment. "But next weekend, your ass is mine."

"Maria, sweetheart, you wouldn't know what to do with my ass," Kyle said with a snort.

"Oh yes I do. I'm gonna take that fine ass out dancing so you can make me look good." Maria's grin was decidedly evil.

After brunch, Maria decided to come along with him to check in on his aunt Ollie. She had just moved into a new retirement community, and Kyle was anxious to see how she was getting on. Luckily for him, Maria loved his aunt as much as he did. The two women had clicked as soon as Kyle had met Maria in grade school and brought her along for one of his impromptu weekends at his aunt's house. His own mother was always so caught up in her own drama that she didn't notice if he wasn't home most of the time. So he thought nothing of taking the bus out to Ollie's house, his new friend in tow.

As luck would have it, his aunt had gone off to the city for drinks with friends. Kyle had let them in with his key, and they had promptly settled in with a movie marathon. When Aunt Ollie had arrived home to find not one but two children binging on junk food in her living room, she had immediately called Maria's parents. To this day, the "you remember the time we had to call the police because Kyle kidnapped you" story was a classic at every holiday event at the Russell house.

The small room that he walked into was very… beige. He shouldn't be surprised; his aunt had chosen this facility for all the activities and common areas. The room was one area she had decided was not as important. It still depressed him because sterile and bland did not match with her vibrancy.

"It's not that bad!" Aunt Ollie said, obviously reading his face like a book.

"Um, really it is. I mean, I guess I'm just so used to how cheerful your house always was," Kyle said as he looked around critically.

"So make it cheerful for me. Get me some of your lovely photos and maybe some sea glass I can put to sparkle in the windows," Aunt Ollie said with a wave toward the large picture window and then the bare wall adjacent to it. "I've convinced the activity director that we should have a big party for Saint Nicholas Day. I brought all my wooden shoes, and some of the volunteers are scouring the thrift stores for more. You can bring me the beach in my shoe!"

Kyle's mind was already running through his pictures and where the heck to find sea glass. If that's what Aunt Ollie wanted, he'd make it happen. The older woman had been his childhood refuge, and he'd do anything for her.

"Hey, Sunrise Cottage is vacant right now. I know they just finished all the cleaning and maintenance they had planned. You could take a trip and stay there since you have a bit of time off right now. That way you could check up on the work the new maintenance company did this time. You know James has had to change companies a few times already. I'm sure he'd be thrilled to not have to drive down again so soon," Maria said, bouncing in her shoes.

To be honest, heading south to hide in the beach cottage sounded lovely. He had gone to Cape May Point with the Russells a ton of times growing up. They always took a trip at the beginning of the season. At that time of year, the water was still cold, but the town and beach were lovely to visit. The time spent exploring the beach with Maria and James had made every summer special.

"And we used to find all sorts of rocks and stuff over on Sunset Beach. I bet you could see if anyone's found sea glass there too," Maria continued as Aunt Ollie's face lit up.

"Sea glass? Why are we talking about sea glass?" asked his mother as she entered the room, stealing all the joy from Kyle's plans.

"Oh, I just asked Kyle to help me find some pretty things for my room," Aunt Ollie said breezily. "I had not expected you to visit today, Miranda." The unsaid "why the fuck are you here" lay heavy in the air.

"But still, sea glass?" his mother continued, undeterred by her sister's dismissal and oblivious as always to the insult. "I was thinking of what to do next, and I did see a glass blowing class starting up. I'll make you something, Ollie, and I'm sure it'll be better than anything made from sea glass for heaven's sake."

"A glass blowing class?" asked Maria, apparently unable to resist.

"Of course! I think I'm done with my watercolor phase, and it's time to move on to something new. It'll be amazing I'm sure."

Kyle really didn't want to ask, but of course he did. "Did you ever paint that picture I sent you of New York City at night?"

"Oh, darling. I was about to, but your picture just lacked something. I found one by the most amazing photographer, though, and painted that. Randolph just adored the painting, and he hung it up in his entranceway." Yup. He knew he shouldn't have asked. He'd hoped his mother's obsession with watercolor would give him a bridge to something they could share. Sadly, even in this she had to find a way to be better than everyone, including him. Especially him. His mother's narcissism was his constant companion in life.

"I'm sure a glass piece would be lovely, dear," Aunt Ollie said. "And we all know how busy you are, so I hate to take any more of your time. I just want to chat with Kyle a bit about the photographs he can bring me."

"Oh, yes, I do have an important meeting in just a bit. But are you sure, Ollie? I mean, Kyle takes perfectly fine pictures, but I can get some for you that are absolutely amazing," Mom said as she headed toward the door.

"That's very thoughtful, but why don't you just concentrate on the glass? I don't want to use too much of your time. And I love to have a little of something different from everyone in the family."

"Well, if you insist. Okay, I will see you all soon. Kyle, are you coming to that gallery with me for the new photography showing Saturday night? The flyer I sent you? I mean, that's the artist who provided the picture I ended up using. You might get some ideas," Mom asked, lingering in the doorway.

"Sadly, Mrs. H, Kyle is already busy that night. I need him to escort me to a fundraiser," Maria said firmly before Kyle could answer. Thankfully. Kyle wasn't really sure if he could answer at this point.

"Oh, dear, you still can't come up with a real date?" his mom asked, then looked at her watch. "Okay, well then, see you all later."

Kyle watched his mother walk out of the room and then

slumped back down into his aunt's guest chair, exhausted beyond reason. His father had left while he had still been too young to remember the reason why, but he was pretty sure he could guess. He couldn't even really blame the man for escaping while he could.

CHAPTER 2

James

"WHAT DO you mean you want to set Kyle up with Brandon?" James asked, trying not to snap at his younger sister. He was glaring at the other end of the hall, where the two men stood talking and looking too adorable for words.

Kyle looked like, well, Kyle. He had fine-boned features that made the word "beautiful" seem inadequate. His hair was purple right now, a deep dark color that set off his light blue eyes. Kyle had a light dusting of freckles that dashed over his cheeks, and James wanted to trace every single one with his mouth. And wasn't that a revelation that had punched him in the gut. Right there in that nightclub six months ago, he realized what he wanted more than anything in his life was the man who had always been there.

"Well, Brandon is sooo cute. And Kyle hasn't dated anyone in forever. So I've asked Kyle to be my date tonight, so I could introduce them…" Maria said, trailing off as she took in James's expression. "Oh my God, you are seriously mad about this. Why are you mad?"

"Because Brandon doesn't have the backbone to be what Kyle needs." James couldn't deny that Brandon was very attractive, in that adorable way that could be extremely hot. He definitely rocked those heavy-framed glasses he wore.

"Seriously? Kyle is wonderful. And Brandon is sweet," Maria protested.

"Brandon *is* sweet. And Kyle's mother will have him running for the hills. You know this. So why are you setting that poor boy up for failure? And Kyle doesn't need yet another guy bailing on him," James said, irate all over again.

Maria just stared at him. "I can't believe I'm saying this, but you're right."

"Of course I'm right. I met Brandon last week when you brought him over for dinner, and he's a wonderful guy. But he needs someone to be his daddy." James ignored his sister when she started to choke. "And that's not Kyle."

"Well, I don't think you have to worry about Kyle falling desperately in love with Brandon and getting hurt. He's already giving me his 'get me out of here right the fuck now' symbol," Maria said, catching her breath again.

"I'll handle it," James said, ignoring his sister sputtering behind him. He walked quickly across the dance hall that had been set up for the fundraiser. The informal dinner followed by dancing was hosted by a local group that supported the Youth Recreation Center. And as luck would have it, Brandon was the new director of the center.

James's company helped sponsor a bunch of the youth league teams. True to their sibling rivalry, Maria had sponsored a few teams as well. They had since enjoyed the yearly competition of whose teams would go the furthest into the playoffs. This year Maria had won, and James was pretty sure she had been sweet-talking Brandon to make sure she had a heads-up on him again next year.

"Brandon, it's good to see you again," James said, holding out his hand. As Brandon shook his hand hesitantly, Kyle seemed to pull back. That wouldn't do. He had no idea when Kyle had gone from following him around constantly to avoiding him like the plague, but he didn't like it one little bit.

And he was lying to himself. He knew exactly when Kyle had drawn back. Six months ago, when they had danced at the club. But tonight he had another chance to get Kyle into his arms, and he planned to make the most of it. Nothing in that plan involved letting Brandon get in his way.

"Um, you too. I'm glad you could come tonight," Brandon said.

"Of course! This is a great organization, and I'm glad we could be here to support all the wonderful projects that you have going on," James said. "But if you'd excuse us, I just need to grab Kyle. He promised me a dance, and I love this song."

James had to resist the urge to laugh hysterically at the expression on Kyle's face when he grabbed his hand and pulled him onto the dance floor.

"What are you doing?" Kyle hissed as James began to move him to the beat of the latest South American crossover hit.

"Dancing," James said, earning himself a glare from his partner.

"James!"

"Hey, I'm rescuing you. I gather you sent out the bat signal," James told him. "And, Kyle, you can escape now if you want to. But I'd like it if you stayed to dance with me."

"I sent *Maria* the bat signal! Not you. And it's not a bat signal! Arghhh. Why are you doing this?" Kyle muttered, sounding flustered. Flustered was good. As was the fact that Kyle hadn't already escaped.

"Well, I love this song," James said, then fell silent as he continued to guide Kyle around the dance floor. Kyle gradually relaxed into his arms to James's delight. The feel of a pliant Kyle in his arms combined with the thrumming beat of the music had his every sense on fire. Gradually the music faded, and James held tight to Kyle in the middle of the dance floor.

Kyle was breathing heavily, and his eyes were wide. He looked almost horrified as he gazed up at James before he wrenched himself away and fled the dance floor. James debated following him but decided to allow him his small victory. James needed to get himself under control before he could press the advantage.

James walked over to a small table set up with drinks and downed a bottle of water before leaning against the wall nearby. He pressed his head against the cool surface, trying to get a handle on his chaotic emotions. The thrill of finally having Kyle in his arms again told him everything he needed to know.

"Dude. What was that about?" Maria put her hand on his arm. His sister was almost as tall as him in her heels, so she easily stared daggers at him as he turned around to face her. "I swear, I don't know what's gotten into you. Kyle is my absolute favorite person in the world, and I don't know why you are messing with him."

James sighed and seriously contemplated his choices in life as he closed his eyes and bowed his head. But his campaign to get Kyle to open his eyes to the possibilities between them was a never-ending series of withdrawals. It was time to enlist the big guns, even if it was a blow to his pride. Never mind that Maria would never let him live this down. And still, it would be totally worth it if she could help him out.

"James? You are starting to worry me," Maria said, her tone softening.

He looked at his sister and decided to man up.

"It's Kyle. I mean, of course it's Kyle. But I realized at some point that it's him," James said.

"What's Kyle?" Maria sounded confused.

James wished he had grabbed another drink. Maybe that would've made this conversation less awful. He didn't really know how to put everything in words, but luckily Maria always understood him better than most. Taking a breath, he just let the words flow.

"He's, well, he's everything. I mean he's always been there, ever since you two became glommed at the hip in grade school. And I just took it for granted that he'd be part of our family, part of my life. I'm not as smart as I thought I was. Every time he introduced us to someone special, I always acted like an ass. And every time I thought I'd found the person I'd spend my life with, it never worked out."

"Well, that could be because you kept bringing home Barbie dolls."

"Barb wasn't that bad!" James protested, insulted for his high school sweetheart.

"Okay, point. She wasn't bad or awful or anything else. I still get together with her every once in a while, and she's a very sweet person. But I couldn't live with her without strangling her, I'll tell you that."

"True enough. But anyway, I realized that none of them was ever going to be the right person. Because the right person was already in my life and already part of our family," James said as Maria slowly gazed at him in shock.

"You want to date Kyle?" she asked with a breathless whisper.

"No. Well, yes, but to be honest I want way more than dating. It took me a lot longer than it should have for me to realize exactly how I feel about him. But I've always loved him, it's just that now I realize he's, well, he's who I want in my life. When I'm around him, or at least before things started getting all wonky, life just makes a lot more sense. I smile around him, and I crave hearing what he has to say about all the ridiculous things in his life. I want to protect him from everything that will hurt him. But most of all, I want to kiss him," James said, so there could be no mistake.

"Okay, well then. Let's make this happen," Maria said as she started to beam with delight. "You know that he's always had a crush on you, and I suspect he's running scared now. If you are serious about him, you'll need to own up to your past and explain exactly why you won't walk away from him because you get bored."

CHAPTER 3

Kyle

SUNRISE COTTAGE was a beautiful older home at Cape May Point, with a garage on the first level, and two floors for living space above that. There were large porches on both of the upper levels that provided amazing views of the beach. He sighed with contentment as he entered the main door. This had always been a wonderful place to escape the realities of the world for a bit.

He did a quick survey of all of the living areas, noting all the work that had been done since the last time he had been here. Thankfully everything looked great. It was a vast improvement over the string of neglectful maintenance companies that had been hired to take care of the property recently.

The original company that had tended to the cottage had done a wonderful job for years until the owners decided to sell and retire down to Sanibel, Florida. That had set off a series of never-ending disasters with local companies that didn't measure up to James's expectations. From what Maria had said, James had been coming down regularly to try to get things back in order.

Kyle figured he'd earn his keep right away and sent off a quick update on the cottage. He got back a flurry of over-the-top comments from the peanut gallery. As ridiculous as it was, the fact that he was included in Maria's family's "Yo! Fam!" group chat always made him smile. It was very useful in cases like this as well. He didn't really want to start a direct text conversation with James. He grabbed his gear from the car and stowed it in his normal room at the cottage. His phone rang as he finished stashing his clothes.

"So the place looks good? No unfortunate surprises when the first renters arrive in the spring?" Maria asked.

"It looks just like it should, which I think is a massive improvement. I'll let you know if I discover anything while I'm staying here that needs to be fixed immediately."

"Great! I'm glad it worked out that you could get a few days off. Sounds like getting out of town to spend some time with your camera and beachcombing is just what you needed."

"Yeah, well with that project just finished, it'll be a week or so until I have to start the next one. So it worked out nicely. The timing is a bit tight, but hopefully I'll be able to get Aunt Ollie's gifts done by Saint Nicholas Eve," Kyle said as he checked for the normal stash of items that were stocked in the house. He realized that all the linens were missing. "Oh, and all the sheets and stuff are gone."

"Ah that's right, I think they said they needed to be replaced. I'll make sure they get delivered. Well, I gotta go. Enjoy your trip!" Maria said and hung up abruptly. Kyle stared at the phone in confusion. Maria would usually talk his ear off. Maybe she had a date tonight? But if so, normally she'd make him stay on the phone the entire time she got ready and would send him pictures for his commentary.

He quickly sent her a "WTF" text, then finished stashing his toiletries in the bathroom attached to the bedroom he always used. His phone buzzed, but it was Maria's dad with the instructions to "collect all the things and make them pretty!" rather than a response from Maria. He was pretty sure that by the time he had unpacked and settled in for the night, he'd have a link to fifty different videos on how to make DIY crafts with sea glass from Mr. Russell.

He wasn't sure if Maria was gonna order the sheets and have them delivered or if the Russells had already made arrangements with one of the local suppliers. Luckily he had read the *Hitchhiker's Guide to the Galaxy* as a kid and always had a towel with him. And it was his extra large beach towel, so big enough to use on the bed in a pinch. It wasn't like he was going to go swimming in December.

After he fixed some food and got himself settled, including spreading the towel on the bed (thank you, Mr. Adams), he headed back out to the car with his camera equipment. Sunset would be coming in soon, and he wanted to get a few test shots. The beautiful thing about Cape May Point was that he could get both sunrise and sunset pictures just by going to the different beaches. He had a series in his mind that he wanted to capture, and he had carefully noted down the different spots. It would be almost like a panorama of the sun.

At Sunset Beach, he parked in the lot next to the gift shop. It was mostly deserted this time of year, so parking wasn't a problem. Of course, other times of the year he could just walk or bike over. The Russells had a collection of beach bikes stashed in the shed on the property that were perfect for such jaunts around town. But it was far too cold for that right now.

In the late afternoon light, he started to walk along the beach, his camera equipment slung over his shoulder. He didn't have to walk too far before he set up his tripod to frame the view of the concrete ship in the background, then took a few quick test shots. The sun still hung low in the sky as he concentrated on his positioning.

His eyes caught the glint of a Cape May diamond in the fading sun. The quartz stones would make a nice accent for the window art that he wanted to make. Not that he knew what it would look like yet, but he had vague ideas. He carefully picked up the small stone and put it in the small nylon backpack he had brought along to collect his treasures. His heart raced with excitement when he saw a nice-sized piece of light green sea glass just a few yards up. He found a few others nearby but then ran out of luck.

The whipping December wind had him heading back to the tripod to capture the sun's descent. The richly hued reflection on the water was another thrill. He loved photography and taking pictures of all different kinds of landscapes, but sunrise and sunset shots held a special place in his heart. Ephemeral as always, the sun's rays soon faded, and he headed back to the car.

Later that evening he finished drying off from a wonderfully decadent shower, singing along to his special playlist at full volume. He'd have to tell Maria that the Bluetooth speakers they'd installed in the showers last year were a winner. He wrapped the small gym towel he had scavenged from his bag around his waist before heading to the bedroom.

As he walked, he was debating with himself if he'd try for a sunrise picture tomorrow. He really should, but the temptation to just relax and sleep in was strong. He decided to set his alarm and figured he'd have a twenty-five percent chance of actually getting out of bed. He entered the bedroom, heading to his phone on the nightstand to set the alarm and change his playlist to his normal "evening chill" selection, then froze in fear at the sight of someone looming over the bed.

James freaking Russell stood in the middle of the bedroom,

carefully laying down hospital corners with brand-new sheets. James looked up at him and smiled, his eyes crinkling. Then his eyes suddenly went wide.

"James! What are you doing here? I mean, obviously you are bringing sheets, and this is your house and all that, but why are you here? And I'm naked, or almost naked, and you're in the bedroom, and oh my God I'm gonna shut up now," Kyle babbled, horrified at the words that just spilled out. The tiny, barely there towel covered almost nothing.

James just continued to stare at him, and Kyle's stomach plummeted as he flushed with embarrassment. This. This was exactly what he had been trying to avoid.

"No running!" James said, just as Kyle was looking for an escape route. The man knew him too well. "I'll just finish making up your bed, and then I'll let you get changed. You can even crawl into bed and ignore that I'm here. But don't fool yourself, since you and I will be having a chat tomorrow about that dance. And everything else."

Kyle just stared as James calmly finished making the bed, even putting on the quilts he had gotten out of the hallway closet. When he was finished, he headed back out of the room, passing close to Kyle. He seemed to wait and see if Kyle would stay still or scurry out of the way. Frozen, Kyle just watched him approach. James reached out and kissed Kyle on the forehead before exiting the bedroom.

Stunned, Kyle managed to stumble to the bed. James. James Russell. The man he had lusted after as long as he even knew what it meant to lust. That James Russell had just kissed him. Granted, it was just a peck on the forehead. But oh my fucking God, he had kissed him. As he sat there, he almost reached for his phone to call Maria, but wouldn't that be a weird conversation.

"Your very hot brother, who I've had a boner for as long as I can

remember, is here. And he kissed me. And I'm naked under this tiny towel." And yeah, no. That conversation was not going to happen. Instead he gradually got his limbs working again and changed into his pajamas and did just what James had suggested and crawled into bed.

CHAPTER 4

James

JAMES SAT on the upper porch, gazing out at the beach in the moonlit darkness. The light flirted with the quietly lapping waves, and the sound was one that immediately brought him peace. He realized that he should make more time for this, for coming down to this house when it wasn't filled with summer renters. In the cold of winter, the shore had a different kind of beauty.

This house was filled with memories of eating ice cream at the kitchen table while still dressed in bathing suits before they were all sent outside to rinse off again under the outside shower. The endless adventures of childhood summers, punctuated by the thrill of seeing the dolphins in the water as they swam by as well as the terror of seeing his little sister swept out to sea by a riptide. Luckily she had been rescued quickly by a lifeguard, but the moment was one imprinted on his memory. She had been with him in the water, but she was just out of reach and he had been swamped with guilt. She was his to protect.

Just like Kyle was his to protect. He had always been around, his little sister's best friend and companion in mischief. He remembered that Kyle had been with them that year when Maria had been taken by the sea and had been the one screaming from the shore for her to hold tight, that rescue was coming. Now that he thought about it, he realized Kyle had been wearing a cast on his arm that summer, which was why he wasn't in the water with them.

He smiled at the memory of a frustrated Kyle trying to keep up with the rest of them with the cast getting caught on everything. He had always been the smallest, and still was. At five foot five, he was an odd duckling in their house where everyone was at least three inches taller. James's own height topped just over six feet, and the thought that he could thoroughly wrap Kyle up in his arms made his cock grow hard again.

Just then, of course, his phone rang. He answered, because it was Maria, and he had long ago promised her to always answer the phone. He didn't ever want her to feel that her big brother wasn't available whenever she might need him.

"Hey brat, what's up?" he asked.

"How's it going?" she ground out, frustration in her every word. It was almost enough to make him laugh. Maria was not known for her patience.

"Well, I'm out on the upper porch watching the waves in the moonlight. It's very peaceful. I really should do this more often," James said, barely suppressed laughter in his voice.

"I'm gonna kick your ass when you get home, just see if I don't. How are things going with Kyle, you son of a bitch?"

"Hey now, no calling your own momma a bitch. That's just not right."

"I swear by all that is holy, I will de-gonad you."

"I was putting clean sheets on the bed when he came in the room. He had just gotten out of the shower and was in this little tiny towel," James began.

"Stop! I don't need to hear the blow by blow as it were. 'Cause, ewww. You're my brother, and he's Kyle," Maria said as James began to laugh. "You know exactly what I want to hear."

"Nothing much exciting happened, though I did kiss him on the forehead and sent him to bed. This is a full-scale campaign, sister mine, not a momentary skirmish," James told her.

"Awww, that would be really sweet if it didn't sound like the beginning of a gaming session," Maria retorted.

James had a sudden sinking feeling. "You didn't tell the folks, did you?"

"No, brother dear, I wouldn't do that to you. Oh my God, could you imagine? Dad would start texting all sorts of helpful advice in our family group chat. Can you imagine? Kyle would be mortified."

James groaned. It was exactly what his father would do. Kyle was already spooked, and the wrecking ball that would be his father's attempts at matchmaking would destroy any progress he had made.

"But I will warn you. As soon as they get wind of any of this, they will be beside themselves. Mom and Dad kept trying to set me up with Kyle, just so that they could keep him. The fact that they knew he was gay didn't deter them at all. If they had any inkling that you were even remotely interested in him, they'd have tried something a long time ago I'm sure," Maria said with a laugh.

"That would have been a disaster. Especially if they had tried something right after I came home from college for Christmas break seven years ago and told everyone I was bi. I mean, I have a hard enough road ahead of me now as it is."

"Yeah, you were a cocky piece of work back then. And I think you were trying to date the entire football team and cheerleading squad at the same time. Kyle was not impressed, I'll tell you that," Maria said with a chuckle.

"Yeah, I'm sure he wasn't. And I don't think the parents were either, which is probably why they didn't include me in their 'keep Kyle in the family' plans." James cringed to himself at what an annoying piece of crap he had been that year. So full of himself and his many conquests.

"Luckily for you, brother dear, you grew up. Unfortunately, the parents are as ridiculous as they have always been. If they sound like they are going to pop down for a visit, I will throw myself on my sword for you and distract them with my love life," Maria told him seriously. "But you will owe me, and it will be huge."

"Maria, I already owe you more than I can ever repay for bringing Kyle into our lives," James said, all traces of amusement gone.

"I may have to kill you because my mascara is going to be a mess," Maria said with a sigh. "Good luck, brother. I need to deal with a text I just got in from our new house renovation project."

"Try not to scare anyone with mascara face," James said with a laugh as he hung up the phone. He knew Maria would be all over whatever had come up that required her intervention this late on a Friday night. A few heads might roll, but she would get it taken care of.

She had stepped into her role heading up the family contracting business and had surprised them all with how much of a natural she was. Granted, she had been following their father around as long as he could remember and worked full-time with him every summer since she had been a teen. But they'd all been thrilled that she'd been able to take over so effortlessly when Dad had to pull back from day-to-day operations after a heart attack three years ago.

James had been doubly grateful, as he had never had the same passion for building that his father and younger sister shared. James had fallen naturally into the property management role of handling all the rental properties at the shore that his folks owned when he finished with college. At the time, it had allowed his father to concentrate on the construction business.

James had always helped with that aspect of their lives, and he really did enjoy the work. So much so that he ended up with a small company that handled an increasing number of clients. Luckily he had hired some excellent staff, and the business was doing well. Which allowed him to focus on the one thing in his life that wasn't falling into place.

CHAPTER 5

Kyle

As expected, Kyle killed his alarm the next morning as soon as it went off and promptly went back to sleep. He had spent half the night trying to figure out what the hell was going on. *What the fuck is James doing here? Granted, the man owns the place, but still! The nerve of him to just show up.*

He didn't come to any satisfactory conclusions before he succumbed to sleep. As he finally dragged himself out of bed a few hours later, he was grateful to see the cloudy morning through the window. This much cloud cover meant he hadn't missed a good sunrise photo opportunity.

He pulled on his sweatshirt and walked out onto the upper porch through the sliding glass doors of the bedroom so that he could stare at the beach. Even under the cold gray sky, it was a thing of beauty. As he stood and let his mind wander, listening to the sound of the waves, he was startled by movement just down the street. James was running back to the house, presumably having done his full three-mile circuit up to Sunset Beach, down along Lake Lily, and then over to the lighthouse before heading home.

Kyle watched, entranced, as the man's powerful frame pounded down the street. James looked up at him as he approached the house, then waved at him before he headed toward the door below. Damn the man! The bite in the December wind shook Kyle out of his stupor, and he hurried back inside to get dressed. He changed outfits three times before realizing that he was stalling.

After chiding himself for a coward, he steeled his resolve and went down to the kitchen. There was coffee ready, and a note from James with the word Dilly's on it and a smiley face. Double damn the man. That was cheating. He loved the diner that was their normal hangout in the summers, and it was open on the weekends even in the winter.

He'd barely had time to sip coffee at the kitchen island before James breezed in, freshly showered and changed. He was now wearing faded jeans that hugged his rear and a royal blue long-sleeve tee. The man was drool-worthy, and he had tried for so long not to notice. But now everything was out of whack. Triple damn the man.

"Ready?" James asked, anticipation in his voice. "I have been craving a Dilly's omelet ever since I got in the car last night."

"Um, yeah." Kyle winced at his own fumbled reply. They grabbed their coats and headed out the door, James throwing Kyle off again when he held open the passenger-side door to his car with a bright smile.

Luckily it was a quick drive to Dilly's, and once they piled into the booth with the unnecessary menus, the waitress was there quickly to take their order. Once more coffee was in front of them, James looked at him and frowned. Kyle tensed, waiting for the shoe to fall.

"So, I hope I'm not overreaching, but I was talking to old man

Richardson. Do you remember him? From the house right next to the lake with all the ducks we used to feed every summer?”

"Oh yeah," Kyle replied, some of his tension easing with the reminder of a simpler time. "He has that workshop in the little bamboo forest. He used to let us hang out there for hours and tell us all sorts of stories about the importance of keeping an eye out for the revenuers."

"That's the place. Anyway, what I remembered after I talked with Maria is that he is a very popular artist in the area. I almost forgot about his workshop that was always filled with all things bright and shiny. I looked him up on the web, and he has a ton of amazing art that includes sea glass," James said.

Kyle just stared at him. This was not the conversation that he had expected this morning after what James had said the night before. He had been paralyzed with fear at the prospect of discussing the dance that was seared on Kyle's brain. But they were talking about sea glass?

"Wait, did you talk to Maria?" Kyle asked, floundering for a lifeline.

James just laughed. "Of course I talked to Maria. Have you even tried not talking to Maria? I'm not that brave. But yeah, she told me about Aunt Ollie and the current mission to bring her the beach for her wooden shoe."

Kyle looked at James, startled. He realized that that was exactly what he was trying to do. Bring Aunt Ollie all the shimmering beauty and freedom of the beach. Swamped with emotion, he forced himself to focus on what James had said.

"Wow, he has a website? I'm kinda impressed." The food arrived then, and they tore into their meals with the devotion of true fans, conversation shelved for the moment. Eventually they demolished everything on the plates in front of them.

James stared forlornly at his empty plate, as always looking vaguely surprised that all the food was gone. Kyle laughed at the hangdog expression.

James smiled, then answered Kyle's earlier question. "Yeah, he has a website. You should take a look. It's pretty cool. But anyway, I know you want to make Aunt Ollie something yourself, but I figured he might have some advice or something. He invited us to come by this afternoon."

"Oh, thank you," Kyle said, his heart swelling to know whatever was going on with James, the man still had his back. He always had.

The year that Kyle and Maria had entered high school, James had been a senior. Some guys in his gym class had taken exception to his marvelous attitude and sense of style at the beginning of the year. They hadn't even been original, just crowded him in the locker room and were trying to herd him to the toilets.

Thankfully James and some of his football buddies had come in just then and scared the shit out of the would-be bullies. It hadn't happened again, even after James had graduated. The rest of the football team had made sure that both he and Maria were safe throughout school. Not that Maria had needed a lot of protection, especially after she started field hockey and walked around with that damn stick as if it were a weapon of doom.

"What's that smile for?"

"Just thinking of Maria's stick of doom," Kyle said with a chuckle before he sobered. "And that you have always had my back. You and the entire football team."

James smiled fondly. "I love those guys. And I'm glad they were there for you and Maria when I went off to college. Did you know they gave me updates all the time?"

Kyle groaned. "They didn't."

"Of course they did. I'll have to dig up some of the emails. The time that you put wanted posters up all over the school for the missing sense of humor after they cracked down on the senior pranks was my favorite. That one still comes up when we all get together for beers every once in a while," James said as Kyle hung his head. "Though I do have to tell you that I about lost my mind when Niall messaged me to let me know that you and Maria had gone to one of Brian's parties. I think that was your junior year. I hopped in my car and started driving."

"I think half the team showed up and dragged our asses home to your folks' place. It was so embarrassing."

"Yeah, well, I knew what happened at those parties. No way in hell was I going to let you and Maria get caught up in that mess."

Kyle suddenly realized something. "So that's why you showed up early that morning? I thought your laundry crisis was a bit of a stretch to show up so early on a Saturday."

"Yeah, no. I knew the guys would make sure you two got home, but I had to see you for myself. To make sure you were both safe. It threw me for a loop that you'd do something so reckless. Usually when you and Maria did something outrageous, it was funny rather than outright dangerous."

"I can't even remember why we thought it was a good idea. Junior year was hard, what with Maria's big dramatic breakup."

"Don't remind me. I still want to throttle Heinous Harry." James's grim expression brightened somewhat. "I ran into him at the grocery store this year. I actually called him that without thinking about it."

"Good! I still call him that every time I see him."

"But there's something you're not telling me. Both of you decided to go to that party, despite how dangerous it was. I'm just glad Brian was finally arrested and is no longer a danger. But why decide to go in the first place?"

"I've thought about that a lot. Things had been spiraling for me already that year. Aunt Ollie was spending a lot of time down in Florida to be with her best friend who was dying of cancer. Mom was in one of her 'look at me' swings and everything had to be perfect at home. I was constantly walking on eggshells and I had had enough."

James reached across the table and grabbed Kyle's hand. Startled, Kyle looked up and melted a bit at James's expression. "Kyle, I'm so grateful that you felt comfortable in our home. And that we could be there, even if we might have been a little over-the-top at times. Always know that you are welcome. No matter what, no matter when. I hope that you and I will have something even more, but that's separate from what you already have with our family."

Tears welled in his eyes as he contemplated that. *Our family*. It was the foundation for whatever happened between them.

CHAPTER 6

James

"Wow, THIS is amazing," Kyle said as they walked into the workshop. Mr. Richardson beamed as they headed back to the large workbench that took up the entire back wall.

"I'm impressed it's so warm in here," James said as he stripped off his coat.

"I got the place insulated a few years ago. My old bones don't like the cold much, and I wasn't getting much work done out here over the winter. So Molly insisted I get this place set up for year-round work before she divorced me. Apparently, I was distracting her with all my moping, and she has her own projects," Mr. Richardson said with a wink.

"James," Kyle said, his voice catching. "I know what I want to make."

Kyle was staring at the sea glass laid out on Mr. Richardson's workbench. His eyes were wide with excitement, and his skin was flushed. James wanted to grab Kyle up in his arms and kiss him, but restrained himself. It wasn't time yet.

"What is it you want, Kyle?" asked James carefully, not wanting his voice to betray his desire.

"A rainbow wave. I mean, I guess that's so obvious. But I want to make her a rainbow to make that room shine. With Cape May diamonds as the sun's reflection on the wave."

"Well, then, a wave made out of a rainbow it is! But first, I'm gonna send you on an expedition," Mr. Richardson said with a pleased expression.

"A what?" Kyle asked.

"Well, as you can see, I have a lot of glass pieces right here. But it will mean a lot more if you collect some of the pieces that go in your project yourself. You won't find a whole rainbow on Sunset Beach, but you can find sea glass in a few different colors."

"Oh yes, that's exactly what I want to do. I already found some light green ones and a few Cape May diamonds," Kyle replied.

"Excellent! And you are in luck because there's a storm coming in tonight, which means that the next few days will be a wonderful time for beachcombing. Now, your young man here said that you boys were in town for a week or so?" Mr. Richardson asked. James flushed with pleasure at the description.

Eyes wide, Kyle looked at James. "Um, yeah, I'm here for a week."

"That's perfect. I'll show you a few things around here to give you some ideas. Then you two can go off and have a nice day together and keep each other warm during the storm. Take a few days to collect your treasures from the beach. You two come back here on Tuesday. Once you've settled on your design, we'll set it to polish in the tumbler, and you come back on Thursday and we'll put it all together. Sound good?" Mr. Richardson asked, a broad smile on his face.

"Um, yeah that sounds great. Thank you so much for helping me, Mr. Richardson," Kyle said.

"Oh, it'll be fun. I love doing this, and it's nice to find myself an apprentice. So please call me Stan, and the wife is Molly. You make us feel old with all that Mr. and Mrs. stuff. She'll be grumpy if you make her feel old. And you do not want that woman grumpy! Now you two look around, and I'll be working on a few pieces. You can watch what I do for a bit before you head out."

Mr. Richardson, er...Stan, took out a frame that was backed by some kind of glass and began to carefully piece colored stones into a pattern. As James watched, he was soon entranced by the vision coming together in front of him. Just then Molly came in with a tray of hot coffee.

"Oh, thank you! That smells wonderful," James said.

"You're very welcome," she told him, then turned to her husband. "I'm going to run some of my sketches down to the gift shop this afternoon. Did you want me to bring any of your pieces this time?"

"Yeah, I have some jewelry ready to go," he said as he moved away from his work in progress and started putting together some boxes.

"While he's doing that, would you boys like to go down and see the ducks for old time's sake?" Molly asked with a smile.

"Oh, please? That sounds amazing," Kyle said excitedly. He quickly grabbed his camera and followed her out. James trailed after them, as always amused by the camera that was a permanent fixture in Kyle's hand.

They walked down the bamboo-lined path, and James was utterly charmed. The entire thing was decorated with holiday lights, and even in the daytime it looked amazing. They approached the lake and the ducks swimming on the placid waters. Kyle quickly grabbed some photos, even kneeling down on the grass to capture the oncoming phalanx of waterfowl.

"You're about to get mobbed," James said with a laugh as Kyle quickly scrambled back up as the ducks swarmed him. The ducks took some convincing that they weren't going to feed them and eventually made their way back to the center of the lake. James stood shoulder to shoulder with Kyle as they chatted with Molly about the shenanigans they had gotten up to as youngsters. James realized that Kyle was shivering and quickly snuggled him in closer. Kyle looked startled but didn't pull away.

"Molly, darling, I put a pile of boxes in the car," Stan called out as he approached them through the still-vibrant bamboo.

"And did you have anything else for me?"

"Of course!" he said with a smile as he opened his arms wide. Molly immediately ran up to him, and he picked her up and swung her about, kissing her soundly. James was struck by the open affection displayed by the older couple. Kyle pulled away slightly, and James wasn't surprised to see him steadily taking pictures of the scene in front of them.

Stan was almost as tall as James, with a rugged build and handsome face that made one think of old Westerns. His skin was the burnished color that people with pale skin get after years spent in the sun. He was wearing work clothes that he had obviously chosen for their durability and warmth.

Molly looked like she was about to head into a board meeting. She had on an elegant white coat over a pale pink suit that contrasted with her deep mahogany skin. Her silver curls highlighted vibrant brown eyes. She was slight, even shorter than Kyle. When her husband picked her up, it was a study in strength and beauty.

The couple laughed, then separated. James smiled at Kyle when he finally stopped taking pictures, a slightly dazed expression on his face.

"I'm off. You three have fun! And don't forget to lay in supplies for the storm if you don't have them. The electricity may go out tonight, so be prepared," Molly said before heading back down the path to her car.

They spent the next few hours in the workshop with Stan, as he took them through the steps of putting together one of his pieces. Head swimming, James finally bundled Kyle into his car, his hand full of brochures on sea glass that Stan had given them before they left. Luckily he knew all the spots listed, and this time of year parking and crowds wouldn't be a problem. In the meantime, they had some shopping to do. Molly's words reminded James of some emergency supplies that they should pick up before the weather turned bad.

CHAPTER 7

Kyle

Like most storms this time of year at the shore, there wasn't any snow in the forecast. Just heavy wind and rain and the ocean in a rage. Hopefully all the small craft had returned to the docks, or the local Coast Guard station would soon be overwhelmed with rescue operations.

By the time they entered the house, the wind was whipping at them. They carried the bags in, the emergency supplies from the local store as well as pizza for dinner. James had insisted that pizza was an absolute requirement for emergency supplies, and Kyle wasn't about to argue. They could always stash any leftovers in one of the large deck boxes, and it would stay cold enough. The Russells had always insisted that cold pizza for breakfast was one of the major food groups. Kyle set out the pizza and put away the bottled water and a few of the other food items they had picked up. James had gone to distribute flashlights and make sure all the electronics and battery packs were being charged.

Just then his phone pinged with a slew of texts:

Mom R: *Kyle, Be safe and stay warm and dry!*

Maria: *None of that safe biz. Take a chance! But stay warm!*

James: *I promise to keep Kyle warm.*

Oh. My. God. Kyle looked up as James entered the room chuckling to himself, phone in hand. "What the fuck?" Kyle asked, his pulse racing. Keep Kyle warm? What madness had entered the family chat tonight?

"Pizza!" James cried out. He stole the piece from Kyle's hand and took a big bite. He then looked at Kyle and smirked. His phone buzzed again, and Kyle looked down.

Mom R: *James Evan Russell, you behave yourself.*

Maria: *The full name! You're in trouble, bro.*

James: *Hey, I got us some nice warm pizza. Don't blame me for your sewer brain, Mom.*

Dad R: *Point to James. Now leave the poor kids alone and let them get set for the night.*

James continued to eat Kyle's slice of pizza as he grabbed himself a beer and sat down across from Kyle.

"It's amazing how good this pizza is. I crave this stuff even when I'm in New York," James said.

"Um, yeah, it's good. But you know, only when I actually have some," Kyle groused.

"Oh, no whining. Here." James handed him another slice and a paper plate.

"That was a perfectly fair complaint with no whining involved. Damn, this always tastes amazing. I liked Romero's, though, too. Do you remember that place?"

"Duh. The full-on raid that went down there when we were on our way to go play Skee-ball is embedded in my brain. I don't think I ever saw that many cop cars before."

"And Maria was so upset that we couldn't get pizza there that night," Kyle said, relaxing as they spoke about comfortable topics.

"I thought the cop was going to go into shock when she marched right up to him and demanded that he open the place up for her."

Kyle barked out a laugh. "Yeah, well, at least she didn't have her field hockey stick that time. She always wanted to do everything first. She could have been the first to be arrested at the age of ten."

Silence descended as they made quick work of the first pie. Kyle finally settled back, beer in hand. He stared at James, trying to figure out what the hell was going on. James cocked a brow at Kyle in challenge.

"Okay, we can keep dancing around the elephant in the room, or you could just tell me what the fuck is going on," Kyle burst out.

James sat staring at his beer for a moment before answering. "It's pretty simple actually. You've been avoiding me. Heck, you've even been avoiding Maria in order to avoid me. Which makes me question your desire to remain amongst the living. My dear sister is not one that will put up with that shit for long. She is now demanding that I fix this."

"Fix this? You call what is going on fixing things?" Kyle asked, incredulous.

"Listen, Kyle. All my cards on the table. I got you on the dance floor, and things got pretty damn interesting. Then you ghosted everyone. Finally, when I got you back in my arms at the fundraiser, you looked ready to run again. So. Maria told me about your plan for Aunt Ollie, and it was easy enough to put everything in motion. I hadn't planned on the storm tonight, but that is a nice bonus."

"But why? I don't get why you want all that," Kyle said, frustration riding him hard.

James sighed. "Kyle, I want you in my life. And before you protest that you already are, I don't just mean sitting across from me at my parents' dinner table. I mean next to me in my bed."

"In your bed?" Kyle asked, his voice gone breathy.

"Yes. In my bed. Naked. Maybe tied to it, in fact, so you don't try avoiding me again," James said with a wicked grin.

It was oh so tempting. The idea of James Russell wanting him, wanting to keep him. But that made no sense. James did not keep people. He went through relationships as often as most people changed their underwear.

"James, I won't lie to you. I've always crushed on you," Kyle began, then rolled his eyes at James's smirk. "Yeah, I know, since even your father figured that one out it wasn't exactly subtle. But here's the thing. I can't deny how much I want you. But that threatens everything that I cherish in my life. Once you are tired of me and have moved on to the next person, how do I sit across from you at your parents' dinner table? Because I'm not that strong."

"First, you are so much stronger than you realize. It's one of the things about you that fascinates me so much. Second, like I said earlier, you are always welcome in my parents' home. No matter what. I suspect I'll be the one exiled if anything goes south between us. And third, I know that I've been a major player. But not one single person I took to my bed was you. At some point I realized that it was silly to look for the one person that would complete me when that person was already sitting across the table from me. And that's the most important thing of all."

Kyle just stared at James in shock. And then the power flickered out, plunging them into darkness.

CHAPTER 8

James

JAMES WOKE grudgingly the next morning, the sound of various electronics beeping and complaining. Obviously the power had come on during the night. He started to move, then froze as he felt a warm body snuggle up against him. Kyle.

The old chestnut of conserving body heat by sharing a bed had been a brilliant if overused inspiration. Sadly, sharing a bed was all they had done. The cold bite of the air made taking any clothes off a daunting proposition even if Kyle had been ready for that.

He draped his arm over Kyle and kissed him softly on the top of the head, smiling a bit when Kyle froze in his arms.

"James?" he asked blearily.

"Yes, Kyle. Did you expect someone else?"

"Um, no." Kyle fumbled around to find his phone, which was blaring "Highway to Hell."

"Hey, Maria, yes we are safe," Kyle answered, well versed in all things Maria. He laughed at something Maria said before replying.

"Sure, he's right here." Kyle handed James the phone.

"Hey, brat," James answered.

"So how's it going? Did you get to the beach? Mom was just saying it would be a good day to beachcomb what with the storm and all that."

"Yeah, so Mr. Richardson told us. But no, not yet. We're still in bed," James answered without thinking.

"What?" Maria screeched. "And you were right there next to Kyle? Is there something I should know?"

Kyle snatched the phone back from him as James tried to hide his amusement. He wasn't very successful given the irate glance Kyle shot him.

"Stop it, Maria. It was just cold last night, and that's all," Kyle said, then looked at his phone in disgust.

"She hung up on me," Kyle said. "Your sister is such a pain."

James heard his phone ding and decided that the best idea would be to ignore whatever text had come in. He had a suspicion it wouldn't make Kyle calm down at all. Time for a distraction.

"Okay, so I see the sun. Let's get up and dressed and head to the beach. We are under strict orders, after all," James said, jumping out of bed and pulling the covers off as Kyle griped at him. He ran out of the room, laughing as he headed to reset the beeping electronics and get dressed for the day.

A few hours later, James was entranced watching as Kyle carefully walked down the beach. He had found quite a few pieces of glass and Cape May diamonds to put in his backpack. James had found some as well, but honestly most of his attention was on Kyle and not the far less sparkly things lying on the sand. Kyle had always been a flash of vibrant color in his life, but now he fascinated him on every level.

James was just glad Maria wasn't here to point out how ridiculous he was being. He had finally checked her text earlier, which yes, she had indeed shared with the group. Apparently the "we slept in the same bed to stay warm" line had made her laugh until she almost peed herself. Which, dude, TMI. James clung to the hope that Kyle would continue to ignore his phone while he was on his mission for rocks.

"Do you remember the summer when we were obsessed with finding Cape May diamonds to make that necklace for Mom?" James asked as he bent to pick up a stone that shone translucent in the sun. The quartz stones were a trademark of the beach, and they sold a lot of jewelry fashioned out of them in the store nearby, as well as all over the tourist-geared businesses in downtown Cape May.

Kyle looked up from where he had kneeled down on the beach. "Wasn't that the summer we were determined to find pirate treasure?"

"Yeah, I think Dad came up with the necklace idea so that we wouldn't destroy the beach in our search," James laughed.

"We should get your mom some stones too," Kyle said. "We can polish them with the others, and maybe you can make something while I'm working on my rainbow. I think Stan had some simple jewelry settings." James reached down to help Kyle up before he kissed him lightly on the forehead.

"Um, what was that for?" Kyle asked.

"For thinking of doing that. Mom will love it. I'll bring everything back with us rather than finishing it here. We'll enlist Maria to help us, and the three of us will give it to her. I guarantee you she'll cry," James said.

"Yeah, she did when we gave her that super glue special that year too. I thought Maria was going to beat us to death when the glue dried wrong and the whole thing fell apart. But she still insisted we give it to Mom."

"I think we're both lucky that Mom figured out how to fix it. She still has it in her jewelry box," James said. "I love the idea of giving her another one. This time maybe we can put it together and everything. I'll see what tips I can pick up from Stan. If all else fails, we'll just drag Maria down here with us and over to Stan's workshop."

"Luckily I've found a bunch of Cape May diamonds already today. You're slacking, though," Kyle taunted him.

"I've been distracted," James said, then reached down and grabbed Kyle's hand. Kyle tensed but left his hand where it was. The tension that had been riding him eased, and the two of them strolled up the wind-tossed beach. The beach was a lively one, festooned with rocks and the flotsam of the tide that had crashed to the shore. Soon enough they were both enthralled by the treasure hunt, and all awkwardness melted away.

CHAPTER 9

Kyle

KYLE STOOD entranced as he carefully took the prepared stones and sea glass, all now polished and ready for use. Stan gave him a nod as he laid them out in the open frame. For right now he was just getting an idea of the pattern, but the next step would be to glue everything to the clear glass at the back. The frame itself was minimal, so the piece should look very much like a wave hung in suspension.

He interspersed his own pieces of sea glass with the other colors that Stan had provided until the overall mix of colors was just right. Then he added in the Cape May diamonds to provide the sparkles on the waves, and he looked up at James and Stan.

"It's beautiful," James said, clasping him on the shoulder. Kyle just nodded, emotions swamping him. It was exactly what he had envisioned, and he'd always be grateful to these two men for helping him.

"Well, then, let's make it happen!" Stan said, and started to guide Kyle through the process of bringing his vision to reality. And he found that he really enjoyed working with the stones to create a pattern. It made him think of all those mosaicists from ancient times and how much joy those artists must have taken from the painstaking work.

After an hour or so of getting lost in all the pretty patterns, they decided to take a break for refreshments and headed up to the house. Kyle brought his laptop with him because he had a surprise for the Richardsons. He sat down in the kitchen with Molly and Stan and opened up his laptop.

"I created an album from some of the pictures I took this week. I'll share these with you electronically, but I wanted to show you a few," Kyle said hesitantly.

Molly smiled as he opened the slideshow with some of his beach shots. "Oh, those are wonderful. So many different angles. And look, there's the concrete ship! I love that sunrise picture."

"It's one of my favorites too," James said with a smile. "But just wait."

Kyle went through the pictures he had taken of the beach as well as Stan's workshop and the lake. And then he got to the pictures of Stan twirling Molly around in his arms. She gasped with delight, and her reaction was a swell of joy in his heart.

"Oh wow. Just look at us," Molly breathed.

"I will get some prints done that you can hang in the house if you like. I have a wonderful lab that I use for processing, and they'll be delivered framed and ready to hang."

"You don't have to do that," Molly began but stopped when Kyle put his hand on her shoulder.

"Molly, nothing would make me happier than for you to take those pictures and hang them in your house. You and Stan have been so generous with your time, and Stan has been a godsend helping me with the sea glass. I don't even know how I would've done all this for my aunt without him. So please, just let me do this."

"Oh, very well. But just look at him. Just as handsome as he was when we first got engaged," Molly said, still staring at the photos.

"How did you two meet?" Kyle asked. He loved to take pictures of people, but the stories were a blessing as well.

"Oh, I've known him forever. He was my big brother's best friend. I was the one who ran interference for them, because our families would've been horrified at how much time we all spent together. But we were just kids, you know?" Molly asked.

"Yeah." Kyle heart clutched because he did know.

"So well, when Stan started treating me differently, I got scared. I thought maybe he didn't want me around anymore. But then I caught him watching me. And his heart was in his eyes. I decided that it was time to stop playing at life and to go for what I really wanted." Kyle caught his breath at her courage.

"Silly woman to want this old man, but there you have it," Stan said as he kissed his wife. Kyle looked over to James, and his heart lurched at the look in James's eye. It was the same look Stan had in the picture in front of them.

Eventually they made their goodbyes, with plans to come back to finish the window glass. Molly was going to let him know which of the pictures she wanted then too. They traveled in silence back to the cottage. It wasn't awkward, but it was filled with the vague sense of beginnings. The late afternoon wind whipped at them as they ran inside. They both froze in the front hallway.

"James," breathed Kyle, looking at him.

"May I kiss you?" James's expression was unreadable.

"Please," Kyle said and then there were no more words. James picked Kyle up and placed him on the small table that stood in the entranceway. The kiss was soft and sweet and everything he could have imagined, but the strength in the large body that had him trapped made him shudder in anticipation. James's breath caught, and he pulled back to look at Kyle's face.

"Are you sure? I need you to be sure that this is what you want," James said quietly.

"And what am I agreeing to?" Kyle's heart was in his throat.

"Well. First, I'm going to take you upstairs to my bathroom. Then I'll take all of these sandy clothes off of you and get you into the shower. Once you are nice and clean, I'm gonna take you to my bed and do wicked, wicked things to you until you don't remember your own name. At the end of the week, we'll drive back and I'll tell my parents that we get to keep you just like they've always wanted," James said.

Kyle tried to blink back the tears that threatened. But James reached out and tenderly wiped away the moisture below his eyes, then kissed him again.

This time when he pulled back, James just stared at Kyle, waiting.

"Yes, I mean, that's all I've ever wanted. To be yours," Kyle said. The time to shield his heart had passed.

James smiled wryly. "And I am yours, Kyle Miller. Don't ever doubt that."

Kyle managed to keep his hands to himself all the way to the stairs, but once they were in the bathroom, he was all over James. Stroking and touching and savoring the man in front of him.

"Enough of that. Let's get you out of these clothes." James reached out to pull Kyle's shirt over his head. In moments, they were both naked under the spray of the shower as James made good on his promise and lathered up every part of Kyle's body before rinsing him off. Kyle closed his eyes and leaned back under the spray, reveling in the feeling of warmth and contentment. Then he gasped in shock and delight as the warm heat of James's mouth enveloped his cock.

Kyle's eyes flew open, and his heart stuttered at the sight of James on his knees in front of him. He groaned as the feel of James's mouth on his cock almost made him come undone right there. James's hands roamed up his legs to fasten on to his ass, and he pulled Kyle in closer, the suction on his cock never lessening.

"James, I can't. It's too much," Kyle said with a whimper as he looked down again, his balls tingling with his impending orgasm. James winked at him, then renewed his attention to his cock, lovingly caressing Kyle's ass with his hands. It was too much. With a harsh cry, Kyle surrendered himself over to his orgasm, his cock spasming in James's throat until he was wrung dry. After tenderly kissing over his shaft and crown, James stood up and took Kyle into his arms.

"I don't remember that being in the planned events for the evening." Kyle rested against James's broad chest.

"Well, I did promise wicked, wicked things," James said with a laugh.

"Ah, but that was in bed. Not the shower," Kyle corrected him.

"True, and I did promise to get you clean in the shower." James proceeded to do just that before drying him thoroughly. Then he picked Kyle up and carried him to the bedroom and laid him out on the bed. James crawled in next to him and turned on his side so he could run his right hand up and down Kyle's body. He had his other arm propped up under his head on the pillow so that he could stare down at Kyle.

"I've always loved having you in my life. Your laughter was like a drug that I was constantly chasing," James said as he continued to lightly caress him, causing Kyle to shudder. "But then all of a sudden I didn't see the boy that I adored when I looked at you. I saw a man, a beautiful man who took what was rest of my heart. And now I have you in my bed."

As Kyle's eyes widened, James reached down and kissed him again. No longer tender and sweet, this kiss was ravenous. His touch on Kyle's body remained feather light and teasing, however, and it was too much and not enough all at once. Kyle pulled back to look into James's eyes.

"It's you. It's always been you for me. Now would you stop teasing and fuck me?" Kyle got out, twitching at James's light touches, needing more friction.

James got up and grabbed a bag from the floor. Positioning himself between Kyle's splayed legs, he reached in for another ravenous kiss. James then sat back, his cock jutting out proudly and capturing all of Kyle's attention.

"Please," Kyle said. "You have no idea how much I want you inside me. How long I've wanted that."

"I will most definitely give you what you want. But first I need to make sure I keep you here, in this bed." James reached into the bag and drew out a pair of shearling-lined cuffs.

Kyle burst into laughter. "Seriously?"

"Yes, seriously," James said with an evil grin before his expression turned serious. "If you don't want this, that's okay too. I just, I mean, for the past six months I've tormented myself with delicious fantasies of what I'd do with you."

"Yes," Kyle breathed, staring at the cuffs.

James reached down and kissed him again, his large body pressing him into the bed. "If you change your mind, just tell me stop. This isn't some scene like in one of those books you and Maria devour. Though I must say I got some excellent ideas from Maria's book collection. This is just for us. If it's not something you like, you have to tell me, and we'll try something different."

And with those words, James grabbed a pillow and maneuvered

Kyle over onto his stomach, his ass in the air. James once again knelt between his legs and then grabbed his arms and cuffed them behind his back.

A shiver ran through Kyle. He felt so ridiculously and exquisitely exposed and vulnerable. His cock twitched in anticipation.

"So beautiful," James said as he caressed his back. "And mine." Then he started to feather kisses over Kyle's back as he massaged his ass.

"Please," Kyle begged. He didn't even know exactly what he was pleading for, except for James. Just for James.

"Shhh. Sexy as it sounds, I don't need you to beg. I'll give you everything you want. Just trust me," James said. And Kyle did. It was a lifetime of trust, well earned in every area of Kyle's life.

James moved his head lower as he kissed the dimple at the bottom of his spine. Then lower and Kyle was moving, light feathers of air over his hole as he murmured words that Kyle had no clue of understanding. Then he began to lick, and precum leaked from Kyle's cock as his whole body tensed in anticipation.

Soothing hands ran over his back as James drove Kyle into incoherency and yet more begging as he rimmed him. He groaned into the pillow as James stuck his tongue into his hole again and again, wracking him with sensation. But Kyle realized that James had slowed, and then he felt him shift. He was about to protest, to cry out, when a slicked finger slid into him. Another finger soon joined the first, causing the stretch in his ass to feel so very good.

"More!" Kyle demanded, trying to thrust up into James's hand, but with his arms behind him, his movements were limited. And then another finger breached him, teasing him open, and he shuddered as he felt everything. James was relentless, stretching him out as he ghosted kisses over his ass.

And then suddenly he was empty, and James was shifting yet again.

"I want you to be able to move for this part," James said as he quickly unstrapped the cuffs, then moved Kyle's arms to his sides, caressing them as he leaned over him. The weight of James above him caused Kyle's cock to leak even more.

The weight moved off him and the sound of foil tearing made his breath catch. Then James was there. Inside him. Sliding inside him as if he was sliding home, and a groan tore from James's mouth as he rested his head on Kyle's shoulder and murmured over and over again just how beautiful he was.

"I know I'm fucking beautiful. Now move!" Kyle ground out, needing James to fuck him hard and fast. Needing to feel James, to feel owned by the man who owned his heart. Needing so very much.

"You're going to kill me," James said, then slid out and back in again, picking up speed when he leaned over Kyle's body and rested his hands on the mattress. He then thrust hard and fast into Kyle. Kyle angled his body up so that he could be filled even more. Relentless, James gave him exactly what he needed until he couldn't think.

James changed his angle and was grazing his prostate with every thrust into him, and it was beyond amazing. Kyle chanted pleas and demands, not even paying attention to the words. James lit every nerve he had as he filled him so wonderfully with his cock, and Kyle was coming, spasming as he was pushed into the pillow again and again. With a hoarse shout, James stilled above him, orgasming into the condom, and just that thought was enough to make Kyle want to come again.

CHAPTER 10

James

JAMES STOOD, huddled around Kyle and trying not to move too much. As the sun fully emerged above the horizon, Kyle stepped back from the camera that was set on the tripod in front of him. He leaned back against James and sighed.

"And done," Kyle said. "That was exactly what I needed to complete the series."

"Does that mean we can crawl back into bed now?" James asked as he hugged him tight.

"Nope. Dilly's," Kyle said. "I'm hungry. And I need coffee."

James whined. He wasn't proud of the sound, but he desperately wanted to go back to bed. They had spent part of the prior evening walking around Cape May looking at all the Christmas lights after a wonderful dinner in town. It was still early in the season, but most of the historic Victorian homes were fully decked out. Some even gave out hot cocoa to guests as they came by. It had been a wonderful evening, but it had been tiring. And he didn't have enough time to get his fill of Kyle in his bed.

"And then we can finish packing up the cars and head north. Everything is pretty much ready to go, and then once we get there we can spend the rest of Friday in your bed at home," Kyle said. "I'll need to process the pictures, but that can wait a bit."

"You say the sweetest things," James said, nuzzling at Kyle's ear, which had popped out from under his hat.

Sadly, once he got home, Maria immediately showed up at his place. As did his parents.

"Sister dear, just because I said we were heading home, that was not an invitation to come over." Maria of course pouted at him until Kyle arrived. He walked into James's living room and froze, as he took in everyone staring at him.

"Kyle, James is being mean to me. Make him stop!" Maria whined and danced out of range with an evil cackle when James lunged at her.

"Children! Don't make me send you all to bed without your dinner," Mom called out, and Kyle laughed. Suddenly, everything was back to normal.

"I want to see your rainbow wave," Dad said, walking over to them.

"I'll show you the picture. Right now it's all packed up tight so it won't get messed up. Stan did it for me, and I don't trust myself to do it again," Kyle said as he set up the laptop on James's coffee table and brought up the picture.

"Oh wow, that looks amazing!" Maria said. "Aunt Ollie is going to love it. Can we see the rest of your pictures?"

And while James was grateful that his family loved his boyfriend–really, he was–they were going to have to stop with the ridiculousness. His mother had her arms wrapped around Kyle as they sat on the couch and looked at all the pictures on the laptop. He seriously was tempted to go over and grab the man and loudly declare that Kyle was his, and the rest of them could just go pound sand.

Of course, just then Kyle looked up at him, tears and love in his eyes. And his heart stuttered to a stop at the thought that this would be their life. Surrounded by family and loved so hard that sometimes it would take his breath away. He looked away for a minute, and Maria walked over and hugged him.

"I know you want him all to yourself, big brother. But he's ours too."

"It's all just so new."

"It is, but you have to suck it up. And yeah, that means being social and all that, rather than dragging him off to bed like you want. But brother dear, before you try and go all caveman and drag him off, just remember that Kyle is and always will be mine. I claimed him first. Luckily for you, I'm willing to share," Maria told him with a smirk.

"Ewwwwww," James replied.

"You know what I meant!" she yelled at him before flouncing off to sit next to their father. James shook his head, then turned back to the couch, wrestled Kyle out of his mother's grasp, and plopped down with Kyle on his lap. His mother looked at him, obviously amused, but went right back to scrolling through the pictures on Kyle's laptop.

"I want some of these pictures too," Mom said as she continued to scroll. "But I think you are right on the six that you picked out for your Aunt Ollie. It will make an amazing series."

"From sunrise to sunset. Yeah, that's the order I have them in too. I'm pretty excited about this."

"She deserves to have all the pretty things in her room. Hopefully after the Saint Nicholas party her place will look like home again."

James knew he still struggled after his aunt had moved out of her old home. The independent living center she was at was highly rated and had seemed to be a great place for her, but Kyle was still having problems accepting it. Since his mother was focused on everything except for Kyle, Aunt Ollie had stepped in and tried to provide him the stability he needed. So, her house was truly his childhood home.

"I'm sure it will be everything she ever wanted, Kyle," Mom said, patting him on the shoulder. "I've heard great things about the facility, and this way she can relax without worrying about all the hassles of home maintenance."

"Are you guys thinking of moving too?" Kyle asked, his voice distressed. For the Russells' home had been Kyle's refuge when his Aunt Ollie couldn't be there. Maria bent down to place a kiss on Kyle's brow as she squeezed his shoulder.

"Oh, not anytime yet. But it's a reality of life, sweetie. Sometimes we have to remember to cherish the people and the memories and let go of the places," Mom said, looking at Kyle.

"Besides, I think our plan when we sell the house is just to go stay in a different one of James's properties every two weeks and see when he catches on," Dad said.

CHAPTER 11

Kyle

Kyle looked at Maria and grinned broadly. The room looked so different with all the color that now surrounded them. All of the pictures were mounted on the walls, and the rainbow wave was hanging in the large window right in front of him. Kyle was supremely happy to see the glass and stones glint in the afternoon sun. The cheerful spirals of light captured everything he wanted to bring into his aunt's room.

The party was raging on in the common room, and he and Maria had snuck in while James kept Aunt Ollie distracted. He had promised to tell her all about their trip to the shore, so Kyle knew that she'd be well and truly out of the way for a while. She had been overjoyed when they had arrived at the center arm in arm and wanted to know all of the details. Well, hopefully not all of them.

"You did good," Maria told him, pulling him up against her.

"It's exactly like I hoped, Maria. The boring walls are the perfect blank canvas."

"Yes, and the color in here now is amazing. But that's not what I meant, you doof. I meant you and my brother."

"I'm still scared," Kyle admitted. "I mean, I love him. I always have. But if this goes wrong, I could lose everything." Even with all the reassurances from James, that was still his biggest fear.

"Kyle, my brother is over the moon in love with you. And no, that's not a guarantee that everything will be perfect. I know my brother, and that rose has some thorns. Or perhaps the thorn has some flowers. I'm not quite sure with him. But there is one guarantee that I can make you. No matter what happens between the two of you, I will always love you, and you will always be part of my family." Maria *eeped* as Kyle tackle-hugged her.

"I love you too. Thank you. For everything," Kyle choked out.

"Hey, you making a move on my man, little sister?" James said from the doorway, laughter in his eyes.

"I will if you don't treat him right," Maria said. "I might even drag out the stick of doom."

"Oh my God, you still have that thing?" Kyle asked.

"Yeah, well, I save it just in case I need to deal with your mother," Maria said with a grimace.

"Um, yeah, good idea. Hey, aren't you supposed to be distracting Aunt Ollie?" Kyle asked James.

"She's thoroughly occupied setting out all the wooden shoes for Saint Nicholas to fill tonight. So we're safe. Besides, I remembered you were going to bring her the beach." James handed him the vial of sand they had brought back.

With a laugh, Kyle put the sand in the wooden shoes that Aunt Ollie had in her living room. They were the same ones she'd used ever since he'd been a child, and he loved the burned wood design on the side. Then laughter spilled down the hallway, and it sounded like the party was coming their way.

"My nephew wandered off, and it's time to leave out carrots for

Saint Nicholas's horse," Aunt Ollie said loudly, just as she entered the room. Her face broke out in a wide smile as she looked around the room.

"Happy Saint Nicholas Eve," Kyle said softly, looking at the woman who had been his refuge. She had opened her heart and her home to him, and he'd treasure those gifts always.

"Wow. You did bring me the beach. This is amazing," Aunt Ollie said as she rushed over to the rainbow wave. "How did you do this? It's just beautiful."

"I had help." Kyle looked at James, who bent down to kiss him.

"Awwww," said the collection of seniors who had entered the room.

James walked over to Aunt Ollie and hugged her. "Thank you. For protecting him until I was able to be there for him. For giving him a home and so much more. Happy Saint Nicholas Eve."

"No, sweet boy, thank you. The two of you together, well that's the perfect gift for an old woman on this day. I've always loved this holiday, as it's about presents from the heart rather than all the trappings. Speaking of which, this is for you both." She pointed to a Wegman's shopping bag sitting on the table by the window.

Kyle caught James's eye, then stepped up to the bag and looked in. With a fond smile, he pulled out a pair of wooden shoes.

"Those are the ones you always used at my house. They used to belong to my father. Though he never got to meet his grandson, I know he would've been thrilled for you to have these. Now that you have your own place, your own life, you should take them with you."

Kyle pulled out another set of wooden shoes. "These I don't recognize."

"Well, those are for James, so you each have a pair. Those used to belong to my mother. She would've adored James and his entire family. So it seems fitting to pass them along as well. The two pairs need to stay together." Joy filled Kyle's heart as James enveloped Aunt Ollie in a huge hug before spinning her around to the laughter of those around them.

Gently, James placed her down before reaching over and kissing Kyle.

"Ewwww. Stop that!" Maria protested, but she was quickly drowned out by the assorted seniors who started chanting, "Kiss, kiss, kiss."

This was his life now, Kyle realized. A sister who had always been an annoying brat but never let him down, a man who owned his heart, and family that loved deeply.

HOLIDAY LIGHTS

After a work crisis, Evan's well-meaning senior citizen neighbors try to set him up for a new career in adult films, but he's an artist first and foremost. A chance meeting leads to a night to remember, though sadly no video to satisfy his wannabe fans.

Axel has no desire for complications in his life. He has friends that are all the family he needs and a career that he loves. But Evan is a temptation that he doesn't want to walk away from. A little holiday magic

CHAPTER 1

He walked through the door of Magee's and let the familiar comfort of home sweep through him.

"Axe!" Harper called and nodded at the small table by the bar. He gave her a wave and headed over, amused when he saw they had upped the game on the yearly holiday decorations. The big wreath on the front door was standard, as were the large Christmas balls that were hung from the rafters throughout the pub. But this year someone had put wine bottles on the tabletops, with green sparkle lights inside. Knowing Harper's dad, they'd probably use the same decorations for St. Patty's day next year.

He draped his bag across a high-backed wooden chair then sat down with genuine relief. He'd put in a long day of work getting his hands dirty, and his muscles were reminding him that he'd spent far too much time behind a desk lately. But he'd wrapped up all the necessary contract negotiations for the upcoming quarter, and the rooftop garden he'd been at today was a spark of joy and a reminder of why he'd gotten into landscape architecture to begin with. He relished the chance to spend the rest of the week with his team there.

"I can't believe how crowded it is tonight," Harper said when she sat next to him.

"Aren't you supposed to be off?" Axel asked.

"Yeah, but we don't usually have a lot of staff on Wednesday. And we're slammed already."

"I suspect it will be like this for the rest of the month. All the events going on downtown."

"Yeah, Da has already updated the schedule for next week. But for now you better be careful or you'll end up behind the bar tonight rather than sitting at this nice comfy table."

Axel laughed. "I don't mind helping out."

"Shhh! Don't say that so loud. If you're helping, then I don't have any excuse not to be pulling a shift."

"Too late, my dear," Harper's father said with a grin as he walked up to them, bringing over Axel's Guinness. He gripped Axel's shoulder for a moment with his massive hand, then headed back to the bar. Axel examined the blank canvas in the glass before him, then drew a Christmas tree in the white foam of the head.

Harper snorted. "What, going to play fancy barista?"

"New career opportunity!" Kyle said as he dropped heavily into the chair next to Axel.

"You look wrecked. What happened?" Harper asked.

Axel really looked at Kyle for the first time since his friend had entered the bar and realized she was right. Kyle did look exhausted. His job at the marketing firm was one he thrived on, but it periodically took its toll.

"Oh, just an extra-long week at work. I can't believe it's only Wednesday. We have a few big projects going on, and one of the high-profile ones keeps trying to steal my artist," Kyle said. "I can't really blame them, but it's making internal meetings a bear to deal with. My current artist is perfect on my team and has no desire to deal with someone else's mess. And I don't want to have to deal with new team dynamics at this stage in my project."

"I think you need a drink." Harper walked back to the bar, greeting friends and family along the way. Her father's side of the family had owned this place for generations. Her mother Jenna, a tall and lovely beauty from Jamaica, had been in the liquor sales business when she met and fell head over heels in love with Kevin Magee.

They'd had three girls and an extended family that rivaled small countries, or so it had always seemed to Axel. But Jenna's heart was enormous, and she'd opened her home to Harper's wayward friends from college, and they had never left. The rest of the family had merely shrugged at their "adoption" and that had been that.

And they had always been there for Axel. When things grew too raw sometimes they let him just be. He didn't have to be happy and talkative and pretend. He'd spent New Years Eve last year sitting on the back porch of their house, the party raging inside, taking comfort from the welcome without expectations. Kevin had wandered out to hand him a drink at midnight, and toasted him silently. The one-sided screaming match that had been his breakup with Ryan on Christmas Eve had lashed him apart, but his family— this family—had helped keep him together.

Harper was making her way back through the crowd, which had grown even more dense, and was jostled into a woman walking past who then stumbled. Axel moved quickly up out of his seat to help steady the woman who had almost crashed into the table.

She was petite, with blonde hair and dark brown eyes, eyes that grew wide when Harper swirled back around.

"I'm so sorry! Are you okay?" Harper asked.

"Um, yeah. Wasn't your fault. I saw that drunk idiot who ran into you," the blonde woman said. Axel looked up to see that Kevin had already intervened and gotten the drunk man to sit at the bar, with what looked like a glass of water in front of him.

"Were you headed to the bar?" Axel asked. He could at least get the poor woman a drink.

"No, not yet. My friend is supposed to meet me, but it's a lot more crowded than I thought it would be, and I'm not sure if he's here yet or not. I was just looking for a table."

"Join us, at least until you find your friend," Harper said, surprising Axel. Then he caught the way she was eying the young woman and rolled his eyes. Harper definitely had a type. "I'm Harper, by the way. Please, sit down."

"Oh, I'm Avery. And thank you," she replied, eyes still glued on Harper. Perhaps Avery had a type as well.

"Sit here," Kyle offered, pulling out his seat. "This way you can keep an eye on the entrance for your friend." After Avery was settled, Kyle slid down onto the bench by the wall, taking the beer that Harper had brought back over from the bar. "I'm Kyle, and the quiet one with good reflexes is Axel."

"Nice to meet you, and thank you all again," Avery started. "Wait, did you say Kyle? You look familiar. Do you work for Banner Marketing?"

"Yeah. I'm one of the Creative Directors there," Kyle said. "Have we met? I'm sorry, it's been a long week even though it's only Wednesday."

"Tell me about it," Avery said with a groan. "And no, don't worry, we haven't met, but I think we were both at a few events, and my colleagues were talking about you. I work over at Esper. Oh, there's Evan!"

Avery waved and caught the eye of someone near the entrance. The man who walked up to the table a few moments later was young, in his mid-twenties, and looked like someone had crossed an adorable twink and a serious Elizabethan gentleman. His clothes made Axel think of foggy nights and cobblestone streets. He exuded sweet from his curly dark hair down to his cute ankle boots.

"Hey Evan," Avery said, bouncing out of her seat to give him a hug, "Got a bit bounced around with the crowd here tonight, and these kind folks let me crash their table. Almost literally."

"Oh, should we find someplace else to go tonight? This place is packed," Evan said as he looked around.

"You're welcome to sit with us," Axel found himself saying, just as Harper chimed in with "Please just grab a seat. I'm afraid you'll find that most of the places downtown will be crowded." Kyle smirked at him, and Axel kicked him under the table. Damn man better step up.

The table could fit all of them, though it was a tight fit. Axel squeezed onto the back bench with Kyle so Evan could sit. Kyle cleared his throat. "So, Evan, do you work at Esper as well?" *Good man.*

"Yes, I'm an artist. Avery and I are on the same team." *Fuck.* As if the man couldn't get any cuter. The artist thing definitely worked for Axel.

"Evan, Kyle here is the one that works over at Banner," Avery said. "You guys got the big Vanex project, didn't you?"

"Yes, and it's a whirlwind for sure. That's not my team though," Kyle said. "What about you guys?"

"We just got signoff on a proposal for a big project from a new client. That's part of why we are out tonight, just to let off some steam," Avery replied. "We're doing the full team party this weekend, though, at Chan."

"That's a great club!" Harper said. "I made Axel come and dance with me a few weeks ago. Kyle ditched us to go on a date, because he's boring."

"I'll have you know I got lucky, and an offer of a repeat, so shut it," Kyle said with a laugh.

"Well, we might make a short night of it," Avery said, looking at Evan.

"Why is that?" Axel asked, concerned by the haunted look in Evan's eyes at that moment.

"Oh, a few of the team are a bit, um, bro frat boys. They make ridiculous comments, and it gets uncomfortable always being in the crosshairs. They never go over the line where anyone else can hear, but it means I can't really cut loose and have fun," Evan said. "And it's even worse for Avery, because they seem to think they are god's gift to women."

"Well, I'm up for kicking some frat boy ass, how about you Axel?" Harper asked. Axel had to laugh. Subtle, Harper was not.

"Um, what?" squeaked Avery.

"Well, I can be your date, and Axel can go with Evan. We get to go out for a night of dancing, and can toe stomp the jerks if needed. Please? I love that club, and taking down assholes is one of my favorite pastimes."

"Haper, remember that they still need to work there before you unleash your wrath," Kyle said with a laugh. "Though if either of you seriusly are looking for work let me know. A few of the teams at Banner are in a bind right now, and I can send along your resume."

"Wow. Um. That sounds amazing. I think I need to think about the job thing, but are you sure you two want to come to a company party?" Evan asked, looking at Axel.

"I'd love to, Evan. Seriously. It sounds like fun, and as Harper said, I can more than handle myself with a few frat bros," Axel said, trying to keep the excitement out of his voice. There were times when he was grateful for his size and strength, and this was definitely one of them. He was more than happy to play bodyguard if it got him the opportunity to go out with the beautiful man. He didn't actually like to fight, but with his build he rarely had to. Most people didn't want to cross him.

"Please?" Harper asked again, full puppy dog eyes in effect and Avery laughed. Harper was no slouch in the size department herself, inheriting her mom's tall frame, and the pitiful look she was sporting was ridiculous on her beautiful face.

"Oh my god, okay. Thank you," Avery said. "Evan?"

Evan looked at Axel without answering, and after a moment the silence was killing him. Then he caught the uncertain look on Evan's face, and it made him want to fix everything.

"You really want to come? As my, um, date?" Evan asked.

"I would love to. Really. It sounds like fun." Axel grimaced at Evan's raised eyebrows. "Okay, the annoying coworkers don't sound like much fun, and company parties usually are about as enjoyable as going to your great-uncle's fifth wedding."

Kyle barked out a laugh. "Oh my god, you suck at this." Axel kicked his so-called best friend under the table before he turned back to Evan.

"As I was saying, I think taking you out on a date to Chan will be fun."

"Even if you have to put up with rude comments?" Evan still looked dubious. "They really are obnoxious. I wouldn't want to put up with it if I didn't have to."

"Yes. I'm used to dealing with Kyle, so I have lots of practice."

"Hey! I resemble that remark." Kyle put his hand out for a fist bump which Harper returned.

"Please? You'll save me from a pitiful Saturday night on my couch," Axel said, going with total honesty.

Evan smiled. "Well, I can't leave you to such a horrible fate. Thank you."

"Hey, put your number in my phone so we can coordinate."

Axel held out his phone, and his breath caught when Evan's hand lingered on his for just a second when he took it.

"Thank you," Axel mouthed at Harper while Evan concentrated on typing in his number. She gave him a wink then turned back to Avery and took out her own phone.

CHAPTER 2

Evan

He needed to go running. In his six months so far in San Diego, he had made time to run until the last few weeks. Weeks he wished he could forget about. So he made himself get out of bed at his normal time, find his running clothes, and go out the door.

That last bit, going out the door, was the hardest when all he wanted to do was wallow and hide under the covers. Or at the very least, hide under a blanket on his couch and binge on bad television. The sad thing was he should be ecstatic. But the thrill of winning the project and the client's happiness with the presentation was overshadowed by the bullshit that was wearing him down bit by bit every day. Damn Jason. For that matter, damn his boss Mr. Hatheway for being oblivious to everything but the project deadline.

As he walked down the stairs, he saw Mr. Liander walking up. The man had to be in his seventies and still took the stairs every day. Today he was dressed up for the holiday, his bright red pants matching nicely with the holly print bow tie he had on over his short-sleeve button down.

"Hey there. Out and about already?" Evan asked.

"Aye, lad. I'll leave the slacking off for when I have no choice. But I walked down to the park to watch the idiots running before dawn."

Evan looked at his own running clothes with a smile for the old man.

"Bah, you are sensible enough to wait for the sun to come up before you go pound your knees into mush. Haven't seen you much recently." Mr. Liander gave him a concerned look.

"Work has been hectic, but the big project is finished." *Thank god for that.*

"You don't sound thrilled." Mr Liander reached out and patted his shoulder. "Is something wrong?"

Evan felt bad for making his drama sound worse than it was. His neighbor was a good man who had taken Evan under his wing when he'd arrived in town. The grand-uncle of an old college roommate, Mr. Liander had found Evan a reasonably priced apartment in his building and had been very helpful. In fact, Evan was a bit concerned what his benefactor would do if he thought Evan was truly in trouble.

When he'd initially toured Serenity Place, he'd thought the complex inhabited by largely senior residents would make for a peaceful existence. He'd been shocked to discover the pot-filled parties and ribald conversations around the pool. This was not a place for the faint of heart, but he also knew that Mr. Liander and the others would have his back no matter what. Given that most of the seniors had very checkered backgrounds, he was trying to avoid any situation where he needed to call on them. Deadly force wasn't out of the question.

"Nothing to worry about. A few of my colleagues are assholes."

"No use wasting your time on lost causes or mean people. If you are looking for a new job, I have a friend in the industry if you know what I mean," Mr. Liander squeezed his shoulder before giving him a wink and stepping back.

"A marketing firm?" Evan asked.

"Well, not so much that, though there is marketing involved to be sure. No, they do those… films. And they are always looking for fresh faces."

"Ha. Well, sadly I am not an actor. Even if I were, there is a lot of competition for real acting jobs." Evan smiled at the elderly man's naivete about the film industry. But he should have known better.

"Not much acting is required in these things. Just a pretty face and a pretty cock from what I understand. You're pretty enough to be in one of those films," Mr. Liander said with a wink.

Evan laughed. Maybe he should be insulted at the suggestion he take up porn, but he'd gotten used to his neighbors' antics.

"I appreciate the vote of confidence. If I can't find anything in my field, I'll let you know," Evan told Mr. Liander. The older man gave him a thumbs up before he headed back up the stairs.

With a smile still on his face, he left the building and began to run, focusing on the rhythm of feet meeting pavement. He was careful not to overdo it after his recent lack of effort, but still sought to lose himself in the physical activity. After a full circuit, he arrived back at the apartment complex, winded and sweaty.

After a quick shower, he dressed and got ready for the day. With the project proposal wrapped up, things would be quiet at the office until they started in on the deliverables full throttle. A few folks had taken several days off, but Evan didn't have many of those yet, and wanted to save them for something fun. Of course, now he might just need it for a job search. At least Jason, who was the worst of them, was headed out of town for a conference he'd been talking about incessantly, so Evan didn't have to worry about dealing with him right away.

Once he got to the office, he snagged a cookie from the plate someone had already put out. The holiday food was going to be the death of him this year. He sighed with relief when he got to his workspace. He had the final images from the proposal pinned to the walls. And they were good. Really good. He couldn't wait to get them refined and see them out in the world. This was the part about commercial art that sang to him. Unlike a painting that might be on display for a very few, his art would be out there for all to see and to appreciate.

"Hey Evan," Jason said from the door of the team room. *Fuck.* And this was why he was even considering that job offer in Denver. He loved everything about being in San Diego, and he loved what he did at his job. But the harassment was never-ending, and he didn't think he could take it much longer.

"Um, hi," Evan fumbled. "I thought you were headed to that conference."

"Of course I am. I have to be there tonight for the dinner. I'll be heading out shortly with the boss. But I'll be back in time for Saturday night. Wouldn't miss that for the world." Jason gave Evan a disdainful look.

"I'm sure," Evan started, but Jason turned and walked away. Well, that had been fairly painless. He checked his email, then decided it was likely safe to go snag some coffee. He grabbed his mug and walked toward the kitchen, and stopped suddenly when he heard the raucous laughter from within.

"Oh!" Avery said as she almost walked into him, where he stood frozen.

"Shhh," Evan said, desperate not to be caught by the mob in the kitchen. Jason would have a ball if he thought Evan and Avery were spying on them. The smell of the coffee taunted him, but he started to turn around to head back to his desk.

"This is going to be epic. Can you just imagine Evan at Chan? I know a bartender there, I'll give him a big tip and get him to drag Mr. Dork out for the dance competition. It's going to be so ridiculous," Jason said with a bark of laughter. "So have your camera phones ready. We'll put together a video for the holiday party. It'll be awesome."

Avery tried to push past Evan, and he gave her a pleading look. When she followed him back to the team room, he took a breath and sank down onto his chair. Avery paced in front of him, and he almost laughed at the idea of drawing her with little clouds of steam puffing out of her ears from the anger.

"Gah, I hate that man. He's so awful, but Hatheway is oblivious. Jason is going to be impossible on Saturday. Are you sure we should go?" Avery asked.

"Yes." Evan smiled slowly. "I think Jason will be surprised by my club attire. And I'll have Axel so I won't have to worry about any shady bartenders." He already knew exactly what he was going to wear. Dorky was not the word for it. Slutty maybe, but definitely not dorky.

"You're right," Avery said, resignation turning to excitement. "We'll have Harper and Axel with us. I can't wait to see them again. And now I really want to see Jason's face when he sees you walk through the door with Axel on your arm."

Evan dropped his head down on the desk. *Fuck. His. Life.* Because yeah, he could picture it too. Axel had been a solid wall of muscle and confidence and had ticked every one of Evan's boxes. His light brown hair framed a face that reminded him of old cowboy movies, and his eyes were a deep blue. Eyes that had looked at Evan with such intensity it had turned him inside out. There's no way he would be able to spend an entire night with Axel without making a fool of himself over the man.

CHAPTER 3

Axel

He stared at Evan's door as excitement raced through him. He smiled in anticipation, his strategy to get to know the younger man better all mapped out in his head.

Then Evan opened the door, and Axel's confident smile was a sad memory as he took in the vision before him. This was NOT a shy, sweet, hesitant creature of refined tastes. This was…*wow*. His brain seemed incapable of working anymore. The man, who he'd expected to be darkly elegant and understated, wore hot as fuck club clothes that could have turned heads on a runway.

"Hi," Evan said with a shy smile as he stepped through the door. Axel almost swallowed his tongue when the man turned to lock the door, his ass perfectly framed in the painted-on black pants.

Axel managed to drag his gaze back up to Evan's face when he spun back around. "Hi yourself. You look amazing."

"Thank you," Evan said as he joined Axel in the hallway. "I love your shirt." Axel's own combination of dress pants and shirt seemed far too tame, though the royal blue shirt drew out his eyes. Which is why he had worn it, and he preened a bit at Evan's compliment.

"I must confess it's one of my favorites," Axel replied. He gestured towards the stairs. "Shall we?"

A wolf whistle greeted them as they walked into the lobby of Evan's apartment building. Startled, Axel looked up. An old man with a broad grin stepped in front of them.

"Well now, you look damn fine tonight, Evan. Did Rick call you and set you up with a test drive? Is this your partner? He looks nice and strong, though I would have paired you with someone with more tattoos. The contrast would be hot as fuck." Axel had to agree with the old fellow, even if he had no idea what was going on. Evan would look amazing next to an inked biker type.

"Rick?" Evan asked, confusion clear in his voice.

"My friend who does those films. I told him about you today, and he seemed eager to bring you on. He said he has the perfect role for you. Something to do with two biker bad boys."

Axel tried not to laugh. He didn't want Evan to think he wasn't taking their date seriously, but damn, who talked like that in an apartment complex lobby?

"Hey, Eric, did you say our Evan here would be in those films we watch every Tuesday night? With all those beautiful young men? That's awesome. You'll do such a good job, sweetie," a cheerful woman who looked to be the same age as the pervy neighbor called over from her mailbox. "Let me know when your first movie is coming out. I have a list of ones that I know I'm going to want to buy."

"Mr. Liander, Mrs. Bloom, stop. I'm just going out with Axel here. We're not filming any porn," Evan said, his face growing red. Axel couldn't stop the grin spreading over his face. The outrageous, and bit scary, neighbors had a point. In that outfit, Evan could step right onto a porn set and have every eye on him.

"Well, if you film it yourself, it's still porn. I'd sure like a copy," Mrs. Bloom said, relentless. "I'll bake you one of those apple pies you like so much, Evan, the one with all the special crumbles on top."

Twilight Zone. That's all Axel could think. Sweet-faced old ladies did not bribe young men with apple pie to get a copy of a home porn video. Just… no.

"That's so sweet, Mrs. Bloom, but no. We're just going on a date. No porn involved. Have a good night!" Evan said, as he grabbed Axel's hand.

"Well, Gladys, I could hook you up with something for some of that apple pie," Axel heard the old man say then joined Evan in practically running out of the building.

As soon as they hit the street, Evan stopped in front of Axel, his eyes wild. "Let's just forget that ever happened. Deal?"

Axel laughed. "No way. I think I need to know what the deal is with this porn career of yours. Especially how you ended up such interesting talent agents."

"Oh, god. My neighbors are ridiculous. But they have been wonderful ever since I've moved in, so I just try to ignore the porn conversations, the togas, and the dubious crime connections."

"Well, I better behave myself unless I want a bounty on my head. Come, I'm parked right around the corner." Axel gestured for them to begin walking.

"Sweet ride!" Evan said as they got in the car. It was ridiculous how happy Axel was to hear that. He had bought the 1968 Mustang convertible as a passion project, the final touch being a candy apple red paint job that had been completed by a friend who was known for her renovation work. It was a tribute to his parents, and it had been important to him to get every detail right.

"Thanks. I'm just glad I get to take her out this weekend. I spend most of my time in my work truck, so this is a special treat. I checked, and they have garage parking there. It seems like Chan is a whole complex. Have you been there before?"

"No. But I was told that I needed to check it out."

"It's a lot of fun. And you're definitely dressed for it," Axel said, purposely looking Evan up and down before he started the car. "Where the hell did you get that outfit?"

"From the last porn shoot," Evan said, and then burst out laughing while Axel choked on his own tongue. "Sorry, couldn't resist. I shouldn't distract you like that while you're driving. Anyway, I did a favor for a college roommate and put together a bunch of concept art and design work for the new club he opened up. Anyway, he got me fully kitted out for Opening Night at his new place while I was still back in New York."

"I didn't realize you were from New York."

"I'm not from there, but that's where I went to college. My family is from Maryland, near Annapolis. What about you?"

"Oh, I grew up not too far from here, then went to Mesa College. That's where I met Harper and Kyle. Afterwards, the three of us stayed. I lost my parents my sophomore year. There's no one else I'm close with in my family, so we created our own with the help of the rest of Harper's family."

"Her family?" Evan asked.

"Yeah, they basically adopted Kyle and me. You'd like them even if they aren't quiet. They love loudly." Axel smiled. "Her folks own the pub, and Harper and her two sisters have grown up working there."

"Three girls, huh? Her dad must have been thrilled when she brought you two home."

"I'll be honest, the first time we went over was hella intimidating. I mean, I'm not a small guy, but her father is huge. And he can definitely take on anyone in a fight. But he welcomed us with open arms." Axel shrugged. "He didn't care that we were gay, or that Kyle wasn't the kind of guy that could lug around a keg. We were a family, and that was it."

"That's amazing. But I'm sorry to hear about your parents. That must have been rough." Evan's voice held a sincere note.

Since they were at a stoplight, Axel looked over at Evan, giving the man a smile. "It was, yeah. And I lost my way for a bit. But my friends were amazing, and I learned to treasure that. To treasure them. And I found ways to move forward. This car is actually part of that. I found an old photo from my parents' wedding, one of those "Just Married" deals with the car all decked out with decorations and signs. They were sitting in an open top Mustang convertible. I remember them telling me stories about that trip, and they had borrowed the car from one of Dad's college buddies."

"Oh, that's so sweet. It's like you have a slice of them still in your life." Evan's words sliced right through Axel, because that's exactly what it was. They stayed quiet for a bit, but it felt right, not awkward. Axel concentrated on the road as they neared the downtown area where the nightclub was located. Traffic was denser here, but luckily the garage he was heading for was well marked.

Once he had parked and locked up the car, they headed toward the stairs down to the street. He took a chance and reached out his hand to bump against Evan's and waited, breath caught in his throat. Warmth flooded him as Evan gripped back, taking Axel's hand in his. And wasn't that amazing. He hadn't been so nervous about holding hands since he'd been in middle school with a massive crush on the star of his soccer team.

"So this is okay? I don't want to presume. I mean, I should have asked before, but are you out to your co-workers? I can just be here as an old friend or something," Axel said, concerned. He'd gotten so caught up in Harper's excitement and the very idea of an opportunity to spend an evening with this man that he had forgotten to set the ground rules.

"It's fine. I mean, I haven't made any announcement or anything, but people know. But you don't have to make things out to be more than they are," Evan said in a rush.

Axel stopped and brought Evan in close to him on the sidewalk. The holiday fairy lights that were strung up in the storefront window cast Evan's face in a reflected glow. His skin was luminescent, and Axel desperately wanted to trace over the smooth surface.

"Yes, I'm here because it seemed like a fun lark at the pub. But don't for a minute think I don't want to be here with you. You intrigue me, Evan. And I think we'll have a good time tonight, and if I'm lucky you'll agree to go out with me again. And if you let me tonight I'm going to hold your hand and hold you close when we dance. I may even kiss you if you like."

"Ooooh. A kiss. That sounds decadent," Evan said with a smile that lit up his face even more.

"Not anywhere near as decadent as I want to be. Not gonna lie here, in that outfit you are making me want a lot of things that wouldn't be appropriate for a team night at the nightclub. But for now, a kiss," Axel said, as he reached down to kiss Evan, sighing with delight as the shorter man reached up to meet him. Their lips touched gently, then Axel pulled Evan up against him as he teased at his lips, opening them up for his exploration.

"Get a room!" came a laughing shout from a car that roared by, and they pulled back reluctantly.

"Yes, I think definitely more of that," Axel said, as they began to walk again, Evan's hand in his. Probably just as well they had been interrupted, but damn that kiss had been intoxicating. His date was sexy as sin, and oh wow. He couldn't wait to see everyone's reaction in the club. Evan's colleagues had no idea what was about to walk through the door.

CHAPTER 4

Evan

The music was a crush of sound as they entered the club. The place was packed, not a surprise for Saturday night. Lights flashed in disco like precision, and in a nod to the holiday season, twinkle lights festooned the balconies above them.

"They said to go to the VIP section on the left of the dance floor," Evan said, almost yelling as they walked right under a speaker system. Axel nodded, and kept a firm grip on his hand as they walked through the club, both of them pausing for a minute as they passed the bar. The entire backsplash was an enormous aquarium with neon lighting, and it was stunning. The fish that swam through the illuminated water were bright flashes of color.

"Wow," Evan mouthed at Axel, who nodded and smiled before heading back on their route.

As they walked, Evan soaked in the energy around him, glad for a sense of the familiar. He'd spent quite a bit of time in clubs like this, and being here felt right. The chaos was a soothing balm to his soul. He'd ignored this part of himself since he'd moved here, his entire focus on his new job, and it had been a mistake.

"Evan!" Avery waved a bottle at him from where she sat at a table next to Harper. She looked relaxed and happy. He did a quick look around, and they'd obviously arrived early, as only a few other folks were there. Thankfully. He could settle in without worrying about Jason and his cronies.

They reached the table, and as soon as they sat down a server was there to take their order. Evan was pleased to see that the uniform was well-made and fit with the theme, the colors matching those in the lights over the bar. Attention to details like that meant the owners of the club cared about a quality experience.

"Parker!" Avery greeted the server with enthusiasm. "We've been pining without you." This section of the club was quieter, thankfully, so conversation was possible without shouting.

"You just want me to bring you more little swords," Parker said with a wink.

"How else will we have a sword fight?" Avery asked cheerfully. She grabbed one of the brightly colored swords that impaled a pineapple in her glass and brandished it at Parker.

"How about you bring Zorro here a water?" Harper picked up her own sword and tapped Avery on the nose with it when she pouted. Okay, that was adorable.

Parker laughed. "And for you gentleman?"

"I'll take a Dark and Stormy," Axel said. "How about you, Evan?"

"Oh, that sounds good. I'll have one of those." It had been forever since he'd had a Dark and Stormy, and it was just the right balance of flavors for his mood. The bite of the ginger beer was much more appealing tonight than fruity sweetness.

"I'll be right back with those. No mutinies while I'm gone!" And with that, Parker was off.

"You two been here long?" Axel asked.

Harper nodded at the small sword collection on the table. "Exactly two drinks." She seemed sober, which made sense if she had grown up in a pub. Unlike Avery, who was well on her way to tipsy.

"Ah, your partner in crime has arrived, Ms. Langham," Mr. Hatheway said as he approached the table. "Good to see you, Evan."

Evan swallowed, then stood to shake his hand and introduced Axel.

"Well, thank you all for coming. Evan and Avery, your contributions really impressed the client and made the whole thing come together. Evan, I'm keen to see what you come up out of that concept art, and I know everyone else is too. In the meantime, have fun tonight!" Mr. Hatheway nodded and headed on to the next table.

"He seems nice enough," Axel said once they sat back down.

Evan knew that was true, and that he should be grateful for it. "Yeah, he is. And he allows people to work without getting in the way."

"Of course, that means half the time he doesn't know what's going on at the office," Avery said.

As if summoned, Jason walked up to the table, a few of his favorites in tow. "Well, well, well. If it isn't our star artist! Hatheway has been nattering on about you non-stop. I even got to hear how brilliant you were at the conference dinner last night." He smiled, but the glare he aimed at Evan was cutting.

Avery widened her eyes. "Oh, that's right. I'd forgotten you went to some conference." Evan tried not to laugh at the fake innocence in her voice. As if everyone in the office wasn't well aware of just how important the damn conference was, and that Jason had been the one going.

"No need to play hard to get," Jason said with an exaggerated leer. "I'm more than happy to show you just how well I can dance tonight. All night." Evan looked around, but of course Hatheway was as oblivious to Jason's misbehavior as always. Brad Jameson, the company CEO, had arrived and Hatheway was busy sucking up.

"Aren't you just charming? But I'm afraid Avery promised me this next dance, so if you'll excuse us?" With that Harper stood up and grabbed Avery's hand, leading her over to the dance floor.

"Now that's a pretty view. Pity," said Tweedledum, leering after Harper as she walked past. He was on a different team at the office, but had lunch with Jason every day. Evan couldn't be bothered to remember his name.

"If you are talking about my best friend, I suggest you keep those comments to yourself," Axel said, standing up. "I don't think we've met. I'm Axel, Evan's date."

Tweedledum just stared at Axel until Parker arrived back at the table, drinks in hand. "Here we are, darlings," he said, as if oblivious to the tension. He gave Evan a wink. "If you need anything else, just let me know. Water, drinks, bouncers. Whatever it is." Then he swanned off, not asking the three newcomers for their order. Evan swallowed a chuckle.

"Have fun just sitting here. We're going to go have some fun and party," Jason said, his eyes on Axel. Without another word, the three of them wandered off.

"Wow. They're special," Axel said.

Evan sighed. "Yeah, the bane-of-my-existence kind of special. I guarantee you at least one of them will forget how intimidated they were just now and hit on Harper before the night is out. They are relentless with Avery."

"Seriously? Why doesn't she complain?"

"Like me, she's new to the company. And they never act like

that in the office. It's only if we go somewhere after hours. And if we say anything, then Hatheway gets all concerned that we're not team players." Evan shrugged his shoulders, annoyance on his face.

"That sucks."

"Yeah, and the worst part is that I love the work I'm doing. This project we just landed is going to be amazing. I've come up with some ideas that will be perfect for the client's vision, and it will be a rush to see my artwork plastered all over the city. Professionally, our team works really well together. Even Jason is exceptional at what he does."

"If any of them touches me, I'm breaking fingers." Harper slumped into the chair next to Axel.

Avery grabbed her water and almost inhaled it. "Oh my god, please? Would you? I'd pay to see that."

"Would you kiss me?" Harper asked, fluttering her eyelashes.

Axel shook his head. "Damn, you have absolutely no game. That was pitiful."

"Okay everyone! Listen up!" Jason had gotten himself on top of a table at the center of the VIP section. "We're going to have a bit of a dance competition, for all the non-wallflowers out there."

Evan groaned as Jason stared straight at him. He wanted nothing more than to show up on the floor and show Jason exactly how wrong he was, but Evan didn't even know if Axel liked to dance. Of course, he had said that he'd been here before with Harper. Maybe he'd lucked out.

Axel leaned in closer and whispered into his ear. "I take that as a challenge." Evan shivered. The press of Axel's body against his was intoxicating.

"You like to dance?" Hope ran through him.

"I love to dance. Shall we show them?" With that, Axel stood up and held his hand out to Evan.

"You four go show how it's done!" Parker cheered as he reached over the table to clean up their glasses. "I'll bring you more drinks when you get back."

"Leave the swords!" Avery shouted as Harper dragged her back to the dance floor.

Axel kept hold of Evan's hand as they followed the women and found a place on the floor. The DJ announced the dance competition to the cheers of the crowd. Jason and his cohort were standing right up next to the stage with women they'd somehow convinced to join them for the competition. Mr. Jameson was standing on stage by the DJ, and wasn't that a surprise. He had his head down looking at something, but his hand had wrapped itself around the other man's neck in a familiar caress. It was fleeting, but Evan was sure of what he had seen. *Okay, well then.*

The rolling beat of the first song took him by surprise for a stutter of a second, then he melted into it. His body moved as the music settled in, and he pressed up close against Axel for a breadth of a moment, then swirled back out again on the chorus of the song. The area around them cleared as dancers were removed from the floor, and Axel expertly maneuvered them around the space.

Cheers rang out as a new song began to play, the Caribbean-laced beats a favorite in New York when he'd been clubbing almost every weekend. He grabbed Axel around the waist and began to grind up against him. Axel moved with him as if they had done this hundreds of times, and the joy of the dance was everything.

A salsa temptation came next, and Evan was able to indulge every last one of his dramatic impulses with Axel anchoring him in the dance. They had all the room they needed for the dance's movements, and the cheering around them got louder. By the time the last note faded and he stood, sweaty and *oh my god*, so needy in Axel's arms, he finally looked around him.

Avery flashed him a brilliant smile from where she stood next to Harper, and he realized that he and Axel were alone on the dance floor. In a rush of movement and sound, the DJ proclaimed them the winners and announced they would get year-long VIP access tickets to the club. More announcements followed, but he couldn't pay attention, too distracted by the man that was still holding on to him. All he wanted at that moment was to have another dance, this one in private.

Sadly, Hatheway insisted on walking back with them to the table, putting a crimp in Evan's plan to slip out with Axel. Jason joined them, and Evan tried not to groan too loudly. At least Hatheway was still there, and Avery was out on the dance floor. And Jason had come alone, Tweedledee and Tweedledum were still dancing with a group of women near the stage.

"Aren't you just full of surprises, Evan," Jason said, eyes fixed on him. "I thought we'd have to bleach our eyes after watching you dance." The laughter was rough-edged, but he hadn't gone over the line.

"Nah, I had a roommate that worked at a club when I was in New York. Spent quite a bit of time there as it turns out." Jason continued to stare at Evan, as if he couldn't figure him out.

"Well, that's just splendid. Always good to see people having fun at these things. And Axel, right? Glad you could join us tonight," Mr. Hatheway continued cheerfully, oblivious to the tension.

"Yes, Axel. I didn't even know that Evan was dating anyone. And then you show up out of the blue," Jason said, then glanced at the dance floor. "And Harper came with a date as well."

"I'm just lucky that Evan invited me," Axel said, tone neutral. But Evan could feel the tension in the man's frame, and knew that Jason was playing with fire.

A cheer rose up, as Mr. Jameson, still standing on the dais with the DJ, announced another competition. Evan could see that Jason was torn, but he stood up and joined Hatheway in heading to the dance floor. If nothing else, Jason was predictable in his desire to suck up, and it gave them the perfect opportunity to escape.

CHAPTER 5

Axel

Harper blew him a kiss as they left the club after one last round of waters brought by the ever-attentive Parker. The damn woman would be all up in his business soon enough, but right now he couldn't care less. He just had to get Evan away from the club and all to himself. While he enjoyed dancing, the whole club scene was something he could only take so much of before he was done. Now, not only was he done, he was beyond himself with need for the man he ushered into his car.

The silence in the car rang in his ears until he turned the car on. The thrum of the motor overrode everything else and calmed his senses.

"Axel?" Evan's voice was tentative, and that shocked him into looking over at the passenger seat. "Is something wrong?" Axel groaned as he took in the sight before him. Evan looked positively debauched, sweat shining lightly on his skin and his clothes clinging to his frame. But he was biting his lip, and Axel's desire took a back seat to sudden concern.

"Wrong? No," he said, putting his finger gently on the lip in question. "But I'm wound really tight right now, and driving is going to be mighty uncomfortable if I keep looking at you."

Evan laughed, relief in the sound. "I think I know something we can do about that."

Axel groaned again. "Yes, so do I. But not here."

"No, not here," Evan said as a crowd of people spilled off the elevator heading to their cars. "You said you lived not too far from here?"

Hallelujah. "Yes. Home it is then."

The drive home was short but took far too long. He offered Evan a drink once he got them in his front door, but Evan took off his shoes then stripped off his shirt and kissed Axel right there in the front hallway under the mistletoe he had strung with ridiculous optimism. The man was sheer temptation, but Axel wanted him in his room, in his bed. So he took Evan's hand and led him through the house.

Finally reaching his room, he tumbled Evan on to his bed and stood transfixed at the sight before him. Shirtless, he looked both sexy as hell and flustered as he gazed up at Axel. His full lips were kiss-swollen and begging for more attention. He swooped down and gave in to temptation, kissing Evan until he heard him whimper beneath him.

At that oh so amazing sound, Axel raised himself up and looked down.

"Are you sure? I won't do anything that you don't want. But if you want, then I have all sorts of lovely ideas."

Evan nodded, and Axel still waited. He needed to be sure.

"Yes, you. I want you."

Axel felt relief surge through him, and stood up and stripped off his own clothes. He grabbed some supplies, then stalked back to the bed, eyes trained on the deep hazel eyes that searched his. He turned his attention to the shockingly toned body beneath him, slowly stripping off Evan's oh so tight pants and the ridiculous strip of a thong beneath. Along with a pair of whimsical reindeer socks.

He pounced on the bed alongside a now naked Evan and went in for another kiss, while he slowly traced over the beautiful body that was splayed out in front of him. Savoring the moment, he kissed his way down Evan's throat and then across his chest before moving lower.

Evan gasped, his mouth opening, as Axel swallowed his cock down to the root before he began sucking and licking until Evan whimpered. Axel brought his hands into play, teasing at thighs and balls, all the while chasing the gasps and moans that were music to his ears.

He toyed and played farther down until he reached the puckered entrance and traced over the sensitive skin. He could feel Evan's body trembling beneath his own. He found the lube bottle and coated his hand, then returned his questing fingers back down Evan's body.

Axel pressed his finger into Evan's body and moved slowly at first before he picked up speed. He paused to add a second finger. Evan keened in desire when he sped back up again, and Axel hummed again around the hard cock that filled his mouth. Evan whimpered, close to coming. Axel licked his lips as he raised himself up and looked into Evan's flushed face, then swooped in and nipped at his lips.

"I need you to fuck me. Please. Just fuck me," Evan babbled.

"Here, roll over." He arranged a pillow beside him and rolled Evan into position. It raised his ass at just the perfect angle, and Axel closed his eyes briefly to regain control.

"I need you to keep your hands right where I put them." He

moved Evan's hands so they grasped the frame at the end of the bed. And with that he swept in with his tongue, licking over the exposed flesh in front of him and tracing a pattern that swept close to the puckered hole and then out again. He nibbled and nipped and then licked ever closer. Evan began to moan softly, spreading his legs ever-wider.

"What is it you want?" Axel asked.

"Fuck me!" Evan demanded, and Axel was happy to hear the confidence in his voice.

"You are so very responsive. What if I were to do this?" And rather than continue to tease and torment he used his hands to spread the man further, and dived in with his mouth, licking at the hot tight entrance in front of him. He licked and laved and let his tongue dive in. The keening moans he was getting were such sweet music, and he kept it going until Evan's cries were getting desperate.

"Please, Axel, please. Need. Please," came the muttered pleas.

"I've got you." He sheathed himself in the condom and slid into the hole he had teased so thoroughly. And pushed himself inside, moaning as he entered the tight heat. He moved inside slowly until he was balls deep in the man. He stopped for a minute, to give them both room to breathe.

"Now!" came the desperate demand. "Fuck me! Move!"

Axel wanted to torment Evan in all the best ways, but he didn't want to make him suffer. He moved his full body to cover Evan's and began to power into him.

"Yes. Please. More! That's it!" The rambling incoherence of the words that met his thrusts were a balm to his soul. He continued to fuck Evan with everything he had. Too soon he felt his balls signal his own impending release. Axel moved his body up further, drawing Evan with him, so he had room to reach beneath him and grasp Evan's hard cock. Evan yelled again and cum flooded his hands after a few quick strokes. Axel's rhythm faltered as the contractions from Evan's orgasm pulled him over the edge. It didn't take long before he gave out his own cry and stilled, his release flooding the condom buried deep.

CHAPTER 6

Evan

Light hit Evan's eyes in a cacophony of brilliance. A rainbow of colors flitted around the room, cast by the crystals hung in the windows which caught the sunlight and exploded it into a delicate dance of beams. The early light reflected over Axel's sleeping face, bringing a softness to his ruggedly handsome features.

He closed his eyes again and groaned. Random hookups were not his thing, and he didn't understand next-morning etiquette. A soft chuckle wrenched him from his thoughts.

"Hey beautiful," Axel said, looking up at him with deep blue eyes. "You're thinking too hard."

"Um, hey yourself," Evan answered, kicking himself for his awkwardness.

Axel levered himself up onto his elbow and then reached down and kissed him. When he pulled back, his warm blue eyes stayed focused on Evan's face. He flushed, uncertain once again of what to do. Was he supposed to make small talk? Thank the man for a wonderful evening, then leave? Awkwardness gave way to pain at that thought. He didn't want to leave and pretend like the prior evening had been nothing more than a hookup.

"Like I said, you're thinking too hard. Relax. We have plenty of time this morning to talk and figure things out. But please stay. I'm gonna go rinse off. I'll be back in just a few," Axel told him and then reached in for a kiss before he pushed himself up off the mattress. "Sleep a bit more, and you can go next. If we shower together, I'll never get to make you breakfast."

Breakfast? The man wanted to make him breakfast? That eased the tension that had been riding Evan as nothing else could. Hookups didn't rate breakfast.

Evan snuggled back into the comfortable pillow as he watched Axel walk away. Damn, that was an amazing ass. He was dozing when the phone rang, somewhere deeper in the apartment. Axel's whiskey smooth voice alerted the caller of his absence through a bluetooth speaker somewhere in the apartment.

"Hey, man, call me and let me know how things went with Evan. I was serious about wanting to poach him for my team, so don't you dare mess things up. Be sure to treat him right!"

As he listened to the end of the call, Evan groaned and stuck his head back under the pillow. He wondered if he would like Denver. Mountains. He liked mountains. Sure, the weather was glorious here in San Diego, but he could get used to the cold and snow again. Maybe even learn how to ski.

The phone rang again, but it was his ring tone. *Damnit.* He looked at the phone by the bedside and let it go to voicemail. He really wasn't ready to deal with any nonsense right now. But as soon as it stopped, it started again. He picked up the phone, staring at the New Jersey number. It wouldn't stop. The calls would come again and again, unless he finally gave into that voice inside him that said just to block the number. For now, he just turned the phone back to Do Not Disturb.

He sat up, gradually stretching as he did so. Muscles protested that hadn't been used quite so vigorously in awhile, and he smiled from the joy from being wanted. He hadn't felt comfortable and safe yet in San Diego, not like he had in New York, where he had found spaces where he could be himself and friends he was sure had his back.

Evan froze, his stretches forgotten, at the sight of Axel striding back into the room, a towel slung low over his waist. Beads of water ran down from his hair and over the broad expanse of his chest.

"Oh, thank god. You're still here." Axel slumped down onto the bed beside him, and Evan longed to lick the water that was pooling on the hair on his chest.

"Um, why wouldn't I be here?" Evan asked.

"I heard Kyle's message while I was showering and didn't...well, I didn't want you to think anything from that. Well, you met him at the pub. He's a bit intense."

Evan started to laugh. "Seriously?"

"I didn't want you to think he put me up to anything. I mean, I wanted to ask you out. I have no idea what he's on about." Axel was seriously cute when he was off-balance. It was a revelation.

"I don't normally get job offers, even second-hand ones, while laying naked in bed. I gotta say it's kind of embarrassing."

"Hey, you're not the one whose ass is being offered up as a job benefit," Axel said, and now Evan couldn't stop laughing.

"Your ass, huh?" Evan choked out before going breathless, the sudden visual overwhelming.

Axel grinned at him, the nervousness from earlier gone. "Is that something you'd like? Because I'd be down for that."

Axel's phone rang again, and he rolled his eyes as he answered. "Go away, Kyle." He stood up and started to pace the room. "No, it's none of your business." More pacing. "Fine, yes. I'll help tomorrow at the pub. And no, I'm not your messenger boy."

With that, Axel flung himself back down on the bed. "Sorry, if I didn't answer he'd keep leaving messages. And I didn't want to have to figure out how to disable the speakers. I'm not used to having guests that aren't family here."

"That's okay. He does seem a bit persistent."

"That he is. Don't get me wrong, I love the man dearly, but he's very determined any time he gets a new idea. Makes him brilliant at his job, but he can be exhausting. Speaking of which, he demanded that I pass along his job offer to you when next I speak to you. I'm ninety percent sure he knew you were here."

Evan gave Axel a reassuring smile. "Um, that's very flattering. I love my job, I really do. The clients that Esper has and all of the history and philosophy of the firm, it's exactly up my alley. I jumped at the chance when the offer came in. I've been considering an offer in Denver, but I'd hate to leave the area now that I've settled in. I mean, Avery is a good friend, and I can't imagine not having the senior mob at the apartments giving me grief every day. If it weren't for the brat pack at the office I'd never leave."

Axel chuckled, though it seemed strained. "The brat pack? That's a good name for them from what I saw. But what about Kyle's offer?"

"I interviewed with both Banner and Esper before I moved out here. At the time, Banner didn't seem like a good fit for me, given the client base and types of projects they do. Much more corporate and less room for whimsy."

"Yeah, I can see that. Kyle loves the prestige of what he does and the clients he works for. Not in a bad way, just that he enjoys the satisfaction of working with the best companies."

"It's definitely a temptation to see that as the solution to all my problems, but I fear I wouldn't enjoy it. And then I'd have to find something else anyway." He'd worked his ass off to get an opportunity to do what he loved, and it would freeze something inside him to give that up just to be stuck in a corporate box.

"I'll just shower and get breakfast ready," Axel said as he headed to the door, his voice strained.

Evan watched him go, trying to figure out what had gone wrong.

CHAPTER 7

Axel

He could almost see the brilliant purple blooms of the peonies nestled next to the pathway, a stunning impact of the color with the deep green of the plants surrounding them. The roof was quiet now, as his crew had already gone home for the day. Now was the time for him to take in everything they'd done and imagine how it would all look in the end. It really would be a sanctuary for the folks who lived in the building, with a winding terraced path through native plants and bushes. The slate pavers would be easy to maintain, as would the benches made of recycled materials.

He had his best crew on this project, and it showed. They'd worked hard, and they would be done before the deadline, which would earn the company a nice bonus that he could pass along to everyone in time for the holidays. The client was using this building as a showpiece for their new investment in mid-height apartment projects, and the roof garden they were putting in would be the centerpiece.

"Hey Axel!"

"Oh, what's up, Sakura?"

"I forgot to tell you that there was an issue with the stair sections. I think we should finish the pavers first, then the rest of the stairs should be here by the day after. It won't be a major change to the plans."

"Oh, ok, thanks. But you know I leave that up to you. You're in charge of the site, I'm just here to be extra labor," Axel said with a smile. Sakura was one of the best that he had, and he trusted her. "I need to go into the office tomorrow, so just let me know if there's anything you need me to do. Especially if the shipment is delayed any further."

Sakura laughed. "Oh, I'll do that. I don't anticipate a problem though. They've never let us down before. This is just the normal last minute scrambling with the holidays coming up. If they say they'll have them by the day following, I trust them."

Axel nodded. "Good. I'm thrilled with how this project is coming along. Roof gardens will make a nice addition to our business here if the idea catches on further. At least with new construction like this."

"I love when our projects allow us to use all of our best ideas. I almost wish we weren't going to be done so soon. Don't get me wrong, that bonus money will be awesome, but I am really enjoying what we are doing here."

Axel smiled at his site supervisor. "I know, and the enthusiasm shows in everything the team is doing. But you know that the next project is going to be a good one as well."

"You're right. It's not as cutting edge, but that museum renovation will be fun. And so many people will see what we do with those garden spaces. I'm gonna bring my grandmother there once we finish. I know she'll love it."

And that right there was why Sakura was his second in command. She loved every minute of what they did and took real pride in their work. With the increase in their business, he was sure she'd be in charge of multiple teams soon enough. That would make his life a lot easier, though he'd still come out to the field as often as he could.

"Go on home, and have a good night."

She nodded. "Yeah, I should. Hot date tonight!" He gave her a thumbs up before she turned back to the stairwell.

In the silence that followed, Axel breathed in the scent of the fresh dirt and mulch that surrounded him. The more subtle scents of flowers teased him with brief bursts of enticement. They had designed the space to be a delight across the senses. Darkness crept over him, though the dim glow of the city that surrounded him with enough light to see where he was walking. The planned lighting would be muted, though clear enough to see in almost any condition.

He stopped by the interlocking block wall, with the view of the city skyline. He looked at his phone again, and the message that taunted him. "Plans for Saturday?" Evan had messaged him yesterday, and he still hadn't answered. Even though Evan hit every one of his buttons, he didn't think he would reply to the text. Better to let this thing between them fade away. Denver. Of all the places Evan could have mentioned, it had to be Denver.

The darkness that surrounded him seemed appropriate. Maybe Evan, with his shiny new job, could hook up with Ryan. That would be lovely. They'd probably get on like gangbusters. After all, Evan had just moved to San Diego not all that long ago. It wasn't surprising he was ready to leave already. Nothing held him to this place. Axel had his life here, his family.

Ryan hadn't understood that. He'd stood there on Christmas Eve last year, full of plans for them to move. He hadn't asked, just assumed. Assumed that Axel would walk away from everything. Move to a new city and start over, because Ryan had accepted a job there. He'd screamed when Axel had asked why he should do that, silencing everyone around them.

Sobs had followed the screams, to be followed by pleading. Why didn't Axel love him enough? Surely they were meant to be. The words had grated against Axel, full of accusation and bitterness. He'd closed his eyes against them as they were hurled at him, not wanting to look at Ryan. Not wanting to look at his family, to see Kevin's quiet sympathy or the indignation of Kyle or Harper.

He opened his eyes now, looking at the city laid before him. Into the blissful quiet. He wouldn't respond to Evan. Wouldn't open himself up to that pain yet again.

CHAPTER 8

Evan

He stared at the laptop screen, frustrated with just everything. Work had sucked. Not that anything bad had happened, but he kept waiting for something to happen and it had him all worked up. He knew Jason's type, heck his older brother was a Jason prototype, and retribution would be coming. His brother and his friends had tracked him down in New York nightclubs just to give him shit. And then invitations to go out had dried up, and he couldn't even blame his own friends for wanting to avoid the whole mess.

So he'd picked up and moved across the country for a fresh start, and now he was thinking of moving again, because he was a god-damned coward. And Axel hadn't texted him back. Even if he was interested in the job at Banner, there's no way he could call Kyle now. Humiliation wasn't his kink.

He had spent all day searching for apartments in Denver. So far he hadn't found anything that excited him. He didn't know if that was just because of his current mood, or if all the locations were truly boring. But really, nothing could compare to this place, with Mr. Liander and Mrs. Bloom and the rest of the pervy senior cohort.

As if summoned, and wasn't that a chilling thought, someone started pounding on his door. Now, staring through the peephole, all he could see was a pie being held up, so he opened the door figuring it was Mrs. Bloom. But as soon as he held the door open, Harper swanned into his apartment.

"What are you doing here? Is this like the Ghosts of Christmas or something?" he asked wearily. He'd be angry, but he just didn't have the energy right now. He'd been unsettled all day, and managed to do nothing while at the same time it felt like he'd ground himself to the bone. Apartment hunting sucked. Feelings sucked.

"Hey now, that's no way to talk to a woman who comes bearing pie. And it's still hot! It would be a sin against our mortal souls not to eat this pie while it's still hot." And with that she continued through his apartment and to his kitchen and started rummaging through drawers and cabinets. He shook his head in disbelief as she very quickly had two slices of pie set up in a tantalizing display on his kitchen table.

"Why are you at my doorstep with a just-out-of-the-oven cherry pie?" he asked, as he sat down and started eating. Cause, seriously, pie. And still warm!

Harper fixed a piercing look on him. "Well, first Axel goes all drama llama on me. And that man is normally so far from tempestuous camelids that it isn't even funny. If it had been Kyle, I would have listened avidly and noted down things I could add to my Twitter feed of 'does this stuff actually happen in real life?' Because that boy can drama. But Axel is the calm and controlled one, who has his life organized and planned out. And you've thrown a spanner into his perfect but boring world, and I may love you a little for it."

Harper looked around. "I need coffee to go along with this conversation and truly awesome pie."

"Are you supposed to call your own pie awesome?" Evan asked as he got up to pour them both some coffee.

"Oh, no, this isn't my pie. I can make world class brownies, but pies are not my thing. As I was headed into the building and was trying to figure out where to find you, I ran into the sweetest old lady. When she gave me directions to your place, she decided this situation had reached threat level pie. Some dude named Eric will have to wait for his baked goods, and apparently, I needed to pay her in porn. Luckily, I have some awesome stuff on my phone, so I'm already paid up." She shoved a forkful of pie into her mouth as if she hadn't just said the most outlandish thing. Well, outlandish to someone who didn't know his neighbors.

Evan closed his eyes and sipped his coffee, then looked at Harper. Now that they were both sitting down, he realized that Harper was a beautiful woman. He'd been so focused on Axel at the pub and then later at the club that he'd somehow missed it. Her eyes were a warm dark brown, and her skin had a wonderful bronze tone Evan envied.

"I still don't understand why you're here. With or without pie."

Harper pointed her fork at Evan accusingly. "Listen, you have Axel in a tizzy. And you have Avery all wound up, since you are her safe harbor at work and she's afraid you're going to run out on her."

"You make it sound like I am getting ready to run away from a shotgun wedding or something," Evan said. "Listen, I don't want to leave the company. But I can't keep working there and having my guard up around Jason all the time. If I wanted to drive myself into the ground from stress, I could have just stayed close to home and dealt with my brother and his friends. I loved New York, but it was too close to New Jersey and my family. I moved here thinking I could escape that kind of harassment."

"So find another job. I know Kyle is super excited about getting another artist on board at Banner." Harper shrugged, and he wanted to laugh.

"Just like that?" Evan asked.

"Just like that. He practically already offered you a job. It's a large company, and if you aren't comfortable working with Kyle, it's unlikely you'd have to."

Evan let out a small sigh as he toyed with his fork. "The thing is, I love my current job. I love what I do, and the clients that we work with. Okay, maybe not all the clients, but you get what I mean. Banner's clients tend to run to the artistic flair I love. Just throwing that away seems drastic. And what about Avery? That won't help her either."

Harper sighed and poked at her pie. "You're right. But are you seriously considering moving to Denver? I don't know why you think that's the solution, but maybe you need to think about that. This is San Diego. Surely there are other firms with the same level of creativity for you. Because it doesn't make sense to me. And honestly, Kyle's firm has more departments that he could probably help you move into something more up your alley."

Exasperated, Evan got up and began to pace. "I just know I can't stay in the current situation. And with Axel ghosting me, even if I wanted to talk to Kyle that would be fucking awkward. I was hoping to convince Avery to come with me to Denver."

Harper sighed. "Did Axel tell you about Ryan?"

Evan stopped. "Who?"

"Ryan. Axel's boyfriend who decided they should get married and move to Denver and live happily ever after. Without consulting Axel. Then got pissed when Axel didn't immediately agree. So you can see how you mentioning picking up and moving to that particular place might have caused Axel to retreat into himself."

Evan made a strangled noise, then Harper continued, "Axel has built a life here. He needs someone in his life who can see that and be grateful for the family that he has. And for that matter, so has Avery."

Fuck. She was giving him puppy dog eyes. He groaned and dropped back into his seat, his head dropping down onto his arm on the table. He wondered if Axel and Kyle knew just how lucky they were to have this woman in their lives.

"I get it, really. But I'll be up front here. Axel isn't returning my texts. And I'm not okay with that. I mean, it's fine if he wants to be done. I can't make him want a relationship. But I'm not going to keep chasing him if he wants to ghost me. I walked away from being desperate for attention a long time ago." Evan was proud that he kept his voice level.

"Oh honey, don't you worry about it. I've got a plan," Harper said with an evil grin that slightly scared him.

CHAPTER 9

He hadn't planned to stop by the pub tonight, but Harper's text had seemed urgent. Kevin normally had the staffing situation down like clockwork, but food poisoning was a thing that could throw off even the best schedule. Time for him to play busboy and keg hauler.

His normal confidence walking into Magee's fled as soon as he spotted the man seated at the table next to the bar. Harper sat beside him, and they had their heads together. *Fuck.* Just as he was considering his option to escape, Kevin looked up.

"Axel! My boy! I didn't know you'd be in tonight." Because of course he didn't. Damn that interfering Harper.

"Do you need any help?"

"Nah, we got it covered. Go have a sit down, and I'll send over some more drinks." Kevin nodded over at Harper, and Axel cursed the fates. He took a breath, then walked over and sat down. Finally he looked at Evan, and his heart skipped a beat at the pain reflected in his eyes.

"Evan?" he asked, confused and hopeful and cursed. Harper stood and walked away, but he kept his gaze focused on the man in front of him.

"I can get up and leave and never bother you again if that's what you want. I tried to convince Harper that you wanted nothing to do with me, but she seems to think we have something to work out."

"I'm not sure," Axel said, desire and despair running through him as Evan bit his lip.

"Well, that's clear as mud. Listen, I don't like to play games. Normally I just back away if someone hasn't responded to me after a few texts. Normally I can take a hint. It's one thing I've learned pretty well in this life. So again, if you want me gone, I'll get up and leave. No need for a scene or recriminations."

"Stay, please," Axel said, guilt flooding his system for not giving the man some respect. "I'm sorry I didn't respond. But I...well, it just seemed easier to let things go." He didn't know how to say this without sounding desperate himself. "I didn't want to start something. I mean, something more than we had already done. Because it was amazing, and I wanted so much more. But you were talking about leaving."

"Yeah. And I'm sorry I just let that all come out. I tend to babble sometimes, especially when things are stressful. I should've been more clear. Yes, I have a job offer in Denver, and yes, it's really tempting to just pack up and go. But that doesn't mean that's going to be my decision. I just wanted to be open and honest about everything that was going on."

"Fuck. I'm sorry I freaked out. It's something I need to work on, but you said Denver and I panicked." Axel rolled his shoulders in an attempt to relax them.

Evan looked over at the bar, then back at Axel. "Yeah, Harper showed up at my apartment and explained."

"Did she now? About Ryan?"

"Yeah. And Denver. And I hope you aren't angry with her. I...well, it's amazing how much she wants to see you happy."

"Oh, I'll give her grief, but no, I'm not angry with her. She's my sister, and I just expect she's going to meddle. I'm kinda surprised you let her in to explain things to you."

"She cheated." Evan flushed, and the red streaks on his face were adorable.

"Cheated?" Axel asked, intrigued.

"She showed up with pie. And it wasn't even her pie! Mrs. Bloom made the pie, and shadowy porn trades were made in the stairwell that I don't want to think too hard about." Evan shuddered.

Axel burst out laughing. "As long as neither of us is starring in them, I think we can safely ignore it. Though Harper in cahoots with your neighbors is a really scary thought. We could tell Harper I'll bring you to the pub and she doesn't need to show up at your place."

Evan smiled, and it was a burst of sunshine. "Does this mean we'll be going places together?"

"If you'll forgive my overreaction and my rude silence, I'd love to have the chance to take you out again."

"Yes. And I promise not to just up and move to Denver. I can't promise that I'll never want to move, but we'll talk about it and I'll be clear about what I want and what the options are."

Axel could live with that. It wasn't a one hundred percent guarantee, but life didn't really come with those. He'd learned that long ago. But Evan hadn't minced words or played games, and he was willing to step out on the limb that bridged the chasm open between them. Axel knew it was a gamble, but he was willing to meet him halfway and see where things went from there.

The real danger was that as he spent more time with Evan, the more he wanted the man. And not just in his bed, though damn that was hot. He wanted to really get to know Evan, and learn all the things that made him smile. Club Evan was different from artist Evan, but both were intriguing and made him wonder how many other facets he could uncover. Which gave him an idea.

"If you're willing to give me that chance, I'd love to take you out tomorrow night," Axel said.

"Tomorrow is Sunday. Are you sure? I know Mondays are busy for you."

A thrill ran through him at Evan's concern. "Yes, I'm sure. I'll stop by tomorrow afternoon to pick you up."

CHAPTER 10

Evan

"Let's go find our ride." Axel reached his hand out, and Evan grasped it with a shiver of excitement.

"So where are we going?" Evan was still trying to figure out what made for a Sunday afternoon date. Too late for brunch, and not really a club night. At least not for those who were at least pretending to be an adult, with jobs that demanded they get up first thing Monday morning.

"It's a surprise," Axel said, his grin wide.

"A surprise? That's what you are going with?"

"Yup, sure is. Come along." Axel led him out of the elevator, looking around the entire time. But the lobby was empty.

"You're safe. It's Sunday bingo karaoke by the pool, so we won't get swarmed. It's a big deal. Seats are at a premium, and no one's going to give up a spot if they can help it."

Axel snorted. "Did you say bingo karaoke?"

"That I did." They walked past the gargantuan lighted fake pine tree that had sprung up in the lobby the other night, then out onto the street. Evan realized they were almost to the corner of the main intersection and that the trolley stop was right in front of him. Axel drew him over and looked down the street.

"The trolley?"

"Yeah, it's going to be packed downtown tonight so I thought this would be a better idea. I'd rather not spend most of our evening trying to find a place to park." Just then the trolley pulled up, and Alex handed the driver exact fare for both of them. They had to split up to find spaces they could jam into, but it didn't take long to get to their destination.

As they exited the trolley, Evan looked at the crowds streaming past him towards the waterfront and was delighted. "The Parade of Lights? Really?"

"Really. And we have reservations for five thirty so let's see if we can make it through the crowd," Axel said as he grabbed Evan's hand once again to lead him through the festive crowd. It was still daylight out, but people were already wearing light-up decorations of every kind. Axel didn't let go of Evan's hand the entire time they walked along the waterfront. People were dashing this way and that trying to get a good vantage point. The carnival-like atmosphere was infections, and soon enough a crowd that was dancing to ridiculously bad holiday songs pulled them into the fray.

Axel spun Evan around in a quick move before bringing him back close up against his body. Wending their way through the dancers, Axel pulled them to the doorway of a stately building parallel to them.

"Here," Axel said as they ducked inside. He made his way to the station at the front of the restaurant where he gave the harried young woman his name.

"Right this way, follow me. I'm so glad you have a reservation. We're being overwhelmed right now by walk-ins who don't understand why the wait is so long." They followed her to a small table overlooking the waterfront. *Damn.* This was the perfect vantage point to see the boats go by. Evan wondered how Axel had been able to score such prime reservations.

"Wow. This is impressive. How did you arrange all this?"

"Luckily I've done a lot of work for people who own things like restaurants, and can usually call someone up if I need a favor. I try not to abuse it too much, lest I end up weeding herb gardens for the rest of my life, but some sacrifices are worthwhile."

"Thank you," Evan said sincerely.

Axel smiled almost shyly. "I'm so glad you agreed to come with me. The first time I saw the parade, it was a wonder. The past few years it seemed like too much effort, and I always had something more important to do."

"So what became more important?"

"Work. I mean, I love what I do. There's so much involved in bringing together my vision for a space, and new landscape architecture techniques keep me on my toes. And I love getting my hands dirty working alongside my teams."

Evan smiled at him. It was a beautiful thing, open and honest. "What's your favorite type of project?"

"Most of my work is commercial, but I love the opportunity to work on parks and public gardens. There's just so much satisfaction in designing a space that everyone can enjoy. And I love green spaces in the city. Right now we are working on a rooftop garden for a new mid-rise apartment building, and it's truly amazing. The people who live there will have an oasis in the middle of the city that's simple to access."

Once they ordered it was so easy to fall into a rabbit hole of conversation, and Axel's love for his work made Evan just a bit jealous. Which was ridiculous, because Evan was doing something he loved as well. The fact that he hated the very idea of going in to work Monday morning was something he needed to fix.

And then the restaurant burst into chatter as the first of the boats went by. The Parade of Lights was as big a spectacle as everyone had said. He sat enthralled as the boats floated by, barely aware of the excellent meal they'd been served. He couldn't believe that Axel had gone to such efforts to take him on such a fantastic date. But as they left the restaurant arm in arm, he let himself enjoy the moment.

Once again, they got swept up in a swirl of parade-goers. This crowd had brought some libations along with them, and everyone was having a wonderful time. As the holiday music played, Axel twirled him around and brought him in for a dramatic dip. Lips covered his own, and he startled when he felt teeth grazing at his bottom lip. He felt himself tremble in the larger man's arms and pulled back so he could breathe again. A cheer rang out from the crowd that surrounded them. Not to mention a few shouted suggestions. Evan flushed with embarrassment, but he couldn't deny the happiness either.

CHAPTER 11

Axel

As he steered Evan through the lobby, the raucous sounds of karaoke bingo from the pool area outside was a horrifying background soundtrack. "Every Sunday?" he asked Evan.

"Yes indeed. Every Sunday. Come rain or shine or alien invasion." Evan cackled at Axel's grimace. "Don't worry, you won't hear it from my apartment unless we open a window."

Axel picked up his pace and bundled Evan into the elevator. They managed to fall into the apartment in record time, Evan laughing when Axel almost tripped over himself in a rush to lock the door.

"Okay, all safe, big guy. No swinging seniors are going to invade. How about you put on a kettle for tea, and I'm going to go hit the shower. I smell like that guy's pineapple drink still."

Axel grinned. "That's your own fault."

"Hey, I didn't trip him." Evan sounded indignant.

"No, he tripped over himself watching you," Axel said. And it was true. The crowds were festive but the drunken revelry stage had definitely set in, and the tipsy man who had been near them while they danced had literally fallen over himself when he tried to follow Evan with his eyes. His drink had ended up in a mess all over the sidewalk, and Evan had managed to step in it as they danced.

After they had both taken off their shoes by the door and Evan walked off to get his shower, Axel was able to find the kettle sitting on the stove and filled it before he poked at the cabinets to find tea. There was a lovely hot cinnamon spice mix right at the front of the cabinet. Once the water boiled, he poured it into the teapot. He inhaled the scent, redolent of holiday indulgence, then stepped back to let the brew steep.

Evan walked into the room just as he put the kettle back on the stove, and he really couldn't think straight. In just a towel, his beautiful body gleamed and tantalized. He walked with a sense of grace that had Axel hard in the breath of a moment.

"Beautiful. You are beautiful. Never doubt that," Axel declared fervently. He hoped that Evan could hear the truth in his voice.

"Um, thank you." The blush on Evan's face was adorable. He decided not to say anything about that.

"Will you come here and let me kiss you?" Evan seemed to square his shoulders then walked over to the where Axel still stood at the counter. Axel took the invitation and kissed him thoroughly, running his hands over Evan's damp skin. Evan shuddered under his touch.

"Oh, sweet. You make me want. But we don't have to do anything tonight. I won't pressure you into anything you aren't ready for."

"I think we already crossed that line last weekend," Evan said with a laugh.

"Yes, but that was before. This is a new beginning." Axel kissed each of his brown eyes, where sparkling droplets of liquid glistened.

"It's so much," Evan muttered, his breath feathering over Axel's cheek.

"Too much?" Axel asked, fear in his heart.

"No, just perfectly enough," Evan answered, and Axel felt tears in his own eyes, gazing down at the man who had stolen his heart and treated it like a treasure. "Come to the bedroom with me?"

Axel shuddered. "Yes." He let Evan take his hand and drag him along to the bedroom. The drawer next to the bed had been ransacked, and lube and condoms were piled on the pillow.

"I want to ride you," Evan said. No games here, just pure desire and want.

Wordlessly, Axel began to strip then settled onto the bed. He splayed out in the middle of the large mattress, and gave Evan his cockiest grin. "Well, have at it."

Evan threw back his head and laughed, and the joy on his face was luminously beautiful. If Axel hadn't already been hard, the sight alone would have driven him over the edge. Everything about this man turned him on.

"I believe I shall," Evan said, and dropped his towel before crawling onto the bed. He took the lube and doled out some on his hand before moving again, nuzzling his face into Axel's groin. Axel groaned as he saw that Evan was prepping himself with his fingers while he slowly took Axel's cock into his mouth. *Damn.* He wasn't going to last long at this rate.

"Oh fuck," Axel said.

"Soon," Evan said as he eased off Axel's cock, then swallowed him back down. This man was killing him. Killing. Him.

Then cold air hit Axel's cock as Evan's mouth popped off. His body protested, but before Axel could say anything, he heard the tear of the foil packet and Evan deftly sheathed his cock with the condom. Then Evan was there, sinking down onto him. And sweet hell, was that a sight. Those hazel eyes were closed, but his curly dark hair was thrown back, the line of his neck a lickable expanse.

But Axel sensed Evan's need, and didn't move to reach for him. Instead he lay back, and let the man ride as he had asked.

"Touch me," Evan said, as his body began to move, to take Axel's cock in at increasing speed that had his nerves singing with pleasure.

"Like this?" Axel asked, reaching up to trace over that exposed neck.

"No," Evan said.

"Like this?" Axel moved his fingers to swirl over Evan's nipples, flicking them then circling as Evan panted with desire.

"No," Evan said, his voice rough and shaky. "Touch my cock. Stroke it, stroke me."

Axel slowly moved his hands down Evan's torso, and Evan growled, but he didn't stop the rhythm that he'd set, continuing to take Axel into his body with desperate speed. Axel wanted to give him everything, everything he'd asked for, everything he needed. And wasn't that a thought. For now, though, he could give him pleasure.

He blindly reached for the lube, then he took his slicked hand and cupped it around Evan's cock where it pistoned over him, grasping him more firmly once he had settled into the dance Evan set for them both.

"Fuck, yeah. More," Evan said, his movements starting to stutter a bit, his eyes wide and fastened on Axel's face. And that was it. He felt the heat in his balls, and the rush of feeling from his spine as his own release was almost on him. He put more pressure on Evan's cock as he stroked him off.

"Now, Evan," he growled out, his body screaming at him for release and Evan's movements ever more frantic. Cum suddenly soaked his hand, soaked his groin and Axel grasped Evan around the waist to keep him still as he shouted out, his own climax washing over him.

CHAPTER 12

Evan

He woke up slowly and felt the arm that was draped around his waist. He turned his head and met the beautiful eyes that stared into his.

Axel gave him a lazy smile. "There you are, beautiful. Good morning. I'm gonna have to run, but I wanted a morning kiss."

"A kiss you can have. I think there's still some pie left too we can use for a quick breakfast."

"You have talented neighbors."

"Talented and quite frankly a bit disturbing. But they've adopted me, and I don't think I can do anything about it." With those words, Evan felt something settle in his heart.

"Likely not. Just don't let them drag you into a career in porn. Not even for more pie," Axel said.

"But the pie is good!" Evan protested, laughing.

"Yeah, it is. But your neighbors are still scary." Axel swooped in for a kiss, then let him go.

"I'm glad you stayed." Evan stood up and found his slippers

before heading toward the kitchen. He grabbed a few plates and set them out.

"I'm glad I stayed too," Axel said as he bracketed his hands on either side of Evan's head and kissed him while grinding into him. The passion was unmistakable. While Evan still doubted many things, he had no doubt at all about the desire he saw on Axel's face. He already knew he could trust Axel with his body. He was starting to realize he could trust him with his heart too.

Later that morning, his heart still full to bursting, he walked into the office. The quiet buzz was less chaotic than normal, as everyone wound down toward the holidays. He knew everything would have a much more urgent feel to it at the beginning of January, as new projects kicked off. Projects like the one he was working on. He was happy to have this time to slowly work through some ideas he had before the pressure kicked up.

He'd managed to lose himself in the drawings he was doing at his desk. He had all the presentation materials laid out around him from the big proposal and was working on a fragment of an idea. It was mostly feeling and intent right now, but he was coaxing it forward.

"Hey clubbie," Jason said to the chuckles of his cohort. Really? They'd called him that all week, and it was just silly. He'd been called far worse, but they seemed to think they were hysterical.

Evan turned around, knowing that ignoring Jason would just make it worse. "Hi Jason. Just trying to get some things down on paper, and I'm in a bit of a roll. So how about we touch base later?" It was worth a try.

Jason and the others entered the room and sat at the conference table set up in the center. "You know, I heard Hatheway just telling the big bosses the other day about how key your drawings were to the big sales proposal." Evan tried not to groan. Jason would never let that go. Even though he needed Evan and the rest of the team to make everything work, Jason was supposed to be the golden boy. The one whose name came up in conversation with the executives.

"So I have to wonder, clubbie, just who did you blow? Did you corner Hatheway at the club? Or maybe in his office? I bet you drop to your knees like a champ, don't you?" All three of them laughed, and it had an ugly sound to it.

"Gentleman, I suggest that you stop talking and walk with me to my office. Evan, stay here and I'll be back to talk to you in just a minute." Startled, Evan looked up to see Mr. Jameson standing in the doorway. Jason looked as if he wanted to say something but then stopped. Jameson's expression was a stormcloud of rage, and Evan would have stepped back himself if he wasn't seated at his desk.

A pall of silence had descended around them, the normal footsteps and hallway conversations had ceased entirely. Evan sat frozen as the three men followed Jameson out of the team room. He stared at the screen in front of him, but the vision he'd been chasing had disappeared in the chaos, and he knew there was nothing he'd get done now. Nausea pushed at him, and a swarm of locusts had taken up residence in his stomach.

He didn't know how long he sat there frozen before he reached for his water bottle with shaking hands, the heavy steel vessel almost too heavy in this fragile moment.

"Evan." The single word pierced through the silence. Jameson walked through the door with Hatheway in tow. Jameson still looked like he was going to use his eyeballs to level buildings, and Hatheway was a mess of fluttering hands and sweat glistening on his brow.

"Close the door," Jameson said to Hatheway before he sank into one of the chairs. He then stared at the fingers steepled in front of him and waited until the door was closed. "As you both know, the Branson project is a huge deal for us. I personally assured Jim

Branson, an old family friend, that this project would be safe in our hands. I know they were impressed with the presentation, and your team deserves kudos for that, Aaron," Jameson said with a nod to Hatheway. "But the piece you might not know is that this project is a trial run. They have a lot of other work that can be ours if we deliver."

This was not the speech that Evan was expecting and he started to relax. Pressure-filled projects were his jam, and he loved being part of something that dazzled the client. Maybe Jameson had chewed out Jason and was here to make sure they could all work together or something.

"I'd heard rumors of problems with the team, but hoped they were false. I didn't have anyone come to my office to tell me of a problem, just outside noise. Jealousy and team rivalry is a real thing, and I'm never inclined to trust the gossip that goes around." With that Jameson leveled his stare on Evan, and he gripped the water bottle even tighter. *Fuck.*

Jameson sighed. "Listen, Evan, I am disappointed you didn't come to me. But I understand why you didn't. It's hard trying to fit in at a new job, and you don't want to be the one to make waves. But I have an open door policy for a reason. I expect that you, and everyone else in this firm, will use it. I'll be making a very strongly worded announcement to that effect later today."

Turning to Hatheway, he continued. "As for you, Aaron, this team is now mission critical and has just exploded in a mess that's been awhile in the making. Because you haven't been paying attention. I'm going to take over direct supervision of this one and pull over a few key personnel to run it. You'll be taking on something else."

When Hatheway started to protest, Jameson shook his head. "Aaron, you've always been a huge asset to this firm, and I haven't forgotten that. It's just that this project leadership needs to be strong right now, and you aren't the right person for the job. Go home, and we'll talk after the holidays."

"Go home? I mean, I have to work that needs to get done before the end of the year," Hatheway said with fear in his eyes.

"Aaron, take a breath. I'm not firing you. Brandy will be in your office when you get there, and you can hand everything over to her. Spend the afternoon together, then you head home and take a break. You look stressed and tired, and this project has been all wrong for you. I'll have something for you when you get back that I think you'll enjoy. Go now, and I'll call you tonight." The two men looked at each other until Hatheway nodded and stood up.

After the door closed behind Hatheway, Evan looked at Jameson. "He didn't know. I mean, he was impressed with the work Jason was doing and encouraged him, but he didn't know all the stuff that was happening."

"Yes, but it should never have happened in the first place. Don't worry about Hatheway, Evan. That's not your responsibility, it's mine. As for the rest of the team, like I said, I'm taking over. Brandy Stern will be the new team lead, and she'll bring a few people with her. Jason and his little clique are gone."

"Gone?" Evan asked.

"They were escorted out of the building and won't be back," Jameson said, then he flashed Evan a devastating smile. The man was a serious silver fox, and Evan briefly wondered if the DJ was a long term thing. If so, that was one lucky man. Then the words sank in, and Evan's breath caught. Gone. They were truly gone.

"And I definitely need you to make sure we deliver on the promises we made in that proposal. It was your art that clinched it, and it will be your art that centers everything we do from now on. Are you ready for that?" Jameson's question was direct and offered him everything he had ever wanted.

"Yes." There wasn't any other answer.

CHAPTER 13

Axel

Harper's uncles were in the corner of the pub, way past drunk, and entertaining the crowd with holiday tunes. Or at least their version of holiday tunes, played on the traditional instruments and with lots of crowd participation. He saw Evan sitting in the normal spot, watching the uncles with fascination.

"Do you think they'd like to come to the holiday party at the apartment complex? They could lead the singing." Evan looked thrilled at the idea.

Harper burst out laughing. "I'll ask them later."

Axel shuddered in horror. "Please no?" Then Kyle was there with their drinks, Avery on his heels. She flung herself at Evan, laughing and crying and Axel exchanged a concerned look with Harper.

Kyle gently pushed Evan and Avery onto the bench at the back of the table so that they could cling to each other without being crowded. Axel picked up his drink, and waited patiently. Whatever was going on was important.

"I have a toast for holiday miracles," Evan finally said, as he and Avery picked up their pints.

Axel smiled at him. "A holiday toast it is then. And what is the miracle?"

"Short version is that Jason and his crew stepped in it at work today, and Jameson fired them on the spot. Avery and I are still on the project, and we don't have to watch our backs at the office."

"Woohoo!" Harper yelled out then chugged at her drink, the rest of them laughing as they followed.

"Seriously, though. You'll be safe there?" Axel asked, thrilled at the hope that bubbled through Evan's words.

"Yeah, the big boss is taking over, and he moved fast. I mean, he brought on some new folks and the whole atmosphere is different. It's all business and teamwork and no frat house nonsense."

Kyle frowned at Evan and then Avery. "Does this mean that I can't poach you? Either of you?"

"Dude, give it up," Harper told him with a laugh. "You know that would just be messy." She reached out and pulled Avery in for a kiss.

"True. I'd have to see that," Kyle said with a grimace as he waved at them, "when you showed up at the office to take Avery out to lunch. I don't think my delicate sensibilities could handle it." Avery blushed at Kyle's words, but extracted herself from Evan and sat on Harper's lap.

Evan reached over and tapped Axel's arm. "I appreciate the offer and the confidence. It definitely helped knowing I had options if things didn't work out."

Axel smiled at Evan, then moved over to the bench to sit next to him. He kissed Evan's cheek and settled in, the warmth of their bodies where they touched a slice of joy.

"So what are you doing next weekend?" Evan asked him as he snuggled in closer.

"Hmmm. I don't have any plans. Why? Going to try and top our last date?"

"I think I was on top that time," Evan said and Axel laughed. "And yes, as magical as the Parade of Lights was, I have something that will blow it out of the water."

"Oh yeah? What's that?" Axel loved to see Evan like this, teasing and confident.

"There will be a party at Serenity Place. Mr. Liander and Mrs. Bloom already told me that they expect you to show up. I told them no cameras, but I don't think they will listen." Axel groaned, then looked at Evan. The man's teasing smile was still there, but there was something tentative and unsure there as well.

"Of course. They are your family here, aren't they? So I'd love to come. And there will be a party here, just for family on Christmas Eve. Will you come for that?" Axel held his breath, hoping that Evan understood.

"Yes. That sounds wonderful." Evan said, his heart in his eyes. And it really, truly did.

"What sounds wonderful?" Kyle asked from across the table.

"Christmas party at Evan's apartment complex next weekend. You should come," Axel told him brightly. "You too, Harper."

"Oh, I'm already invited," Harper said. "That old lady with the pie promised me that there would be strippers and lots of holiday punch." Avery choked out a laugh.

Harper began to sing along with the Christmas Song and then they all joined in. The sound of all the voices raised in song was a rush of feelings every time it happened, and Axel let himself be swept away in it, content to have Evan by his side. This was the true holiday miracle.

BONUS SCENE

You are invited to a holiday party at Serenity Place! Have a little fun with Axel and Evan and all their friends. Please RSVP by joining my newsletter by going to my web page (https://kimkatil.com/) and entering your email address under the Newsletter Signup.

Follow my Facebook page (https://www.facebook.com/Kim-Katil-Author-100560421598444). I'll have a fun contest with one lucky (or not so lucky) winner that gets to crash the party!

On December 24th I will send out links in my newsletter to get the party scene. I hope you come along. If you sign up for my newsletter after the event, you will get a link to access the bonus scene right away!

ABOUT THE AUTHOR

Kim Katil patrols the Universe with her dignity of dragons during the Harvest Moon. The rest of the time, Kim lives in the mythical and contentious territory known as Central Jersey. Originally from South Jersey, she is still unsure if Central Jersey is a real place or a Fae construct. Her movement from the lower to middle band of the state was interrupted by time spent living in Ireland, Boston, Uzbekistan, Maryland, Trinidad, and Florida. So far, she has only been asked to leave one country.

A happily ever after is a necessity. Kim loves to give her characters a fun adventure to get them there and a plethora of family and friends to help them along the way.

She'd love to hear from you on this journey:

Website: https://kimkatil.com/

Facebook: https://www.facebook.com/kim.katil.52

Bookbub: https://www.bookbub.com/authors/kim-katil

www.ingramcontent.com/pod-product-compliance
Lightning Source LLC
Chambersburg PA
CBHW071612150726
48000CB00004B/1701